# "What Do You See?" He Asked.

Andrea traced a line on his palm. "You will live a long and happy life free from worry." Bitter laughter interrupted her, and she looked up. Pain was there in his face, openly displayed in velvet brown eyes. "We are talking of the future, Mr. Collins, not the past."

"So, tell me of the future, gypsy."

She tore her eyes from his and looked back at the palm of his hand, a hand that dwarfed her own. What do I say? she wondered, absently tracing a line. "Your secret hopes and dreams will be fulfilled. You will accomplish what you came here to do. You will be successful and famous." She glanced up through her lashes. Didn't he want fame? "Yet the fame will be on your terms." Now his eyes softened again.

"And love? Will there be a great love in my life, witch?"

She almost giggled at the question. "Yes. You will have a very great romance. Thousands of women will dream of you as their lover." Probably every woman who had ever met him had. "But only one will capture your attention."

"And this one, gypsy? Tell me of this one."

"That has not been revealed yet," she countered. "It will come clear in its own time."

He slowly withdrew his hand from hers. "I think it has already been made clear."

Dear Reader:

Welcome to Silhouette Desire—sensual, compelling, believable love stories written by and for today's woman. When you open the pages of a Silhouette Desire, you open yourself up to a whole new world—a world of promising passion and endless love.

Each and every Silhouette Desire is a wonderful love story that is both sensuous *and* emotional. You're with the hero and heroine each and every step of the way—from their first meeting, to their first kiss . . . to their happy ending. You'll experience all the deep joys—and occasional tribulations—of falling in love.

In future months, look for Silhouette Desire novels from some of your favorite authors, such as Naomi Horton, Nancy Martin, Linda Lael Miller and Lass Small, just to name a few.

So go wild with Desire. You'll be glad you did!

Lucia Macro
Senior Editor

# JANET FRANKLIN

# FREE TO DREAM

SILHOUETTE *Desire*

Published by Silhouette Books New York

**America's Publisher of Contemporary Romance**

**Books by Janet Franklin**

Silhouette Special Edition
*The Right Mistake* #491

Silhouette Romance
*Makeshift Marriage* #691

Silhouette Desire
*Free To Dream* #585

## JANET FRANKLIN

has been writing for years and is pleased that her dream of becoming a published author has finally come true. She is a nurse in her home state of Georgia, and when she isn't busy working or writing, she enjoys music, needlework and reading.

# One

You don't really believe in that do you?''

At the unexpected question spoken in a deep, male voice, Andrea turned and looked up, and then up some more. She replied without thinking as her eyes finally met those of the man who had spoken. "In romance?''

A quiet chuckle rumbled in his chest, and the accompanying half smile crinkled the corners of his brown eyes. "Astrology."

Andrea looked back at the magazine she had been leafing through. It was an astrology magazine opened to her sun sign, but she had responded to the words she had just read. "Romance highlighted this month." "No, I—'' The man was already walking away.

For a moment Andrea stared at the retreating figure. He left the store without looking back, and she put the magazine back onto the rack. For Andrea Jean MacLarson romance ranked equally with astrology. She didn't believe in either one. Both were interesting in an abstract sort of way. It was fun to read astrological forecasts and see what happened. She'd even given in to flights of fancy and had read romance novels. But no, she didn't really believe in romance any more than she did in astrology.

It wasn't until Andrea approached the grocery store that she gave the man she'd seen in the drugstore another thought. When she saw her reflection in the long, glass door she stopped, a grin turning up the corners of her mouth. When she wasn't working, dress was a matter of whimsy, depending on her mood of the moment. This morning her mood had been one of introspection, and her clothes were perfectly suitable for standing at a magazine counter, perusing astrological data.

Her hair was caught back in a black, triangular scarf knotted behind her ear. Long, dangling, bright red earrings, white peasant blouse, black peasant skirt belted with a wide, red leather sash, and red sandals completed the effect. Andrea hadn't thought about her appearance when the man had made the remark, but she could easily have passed for a gypsy fortune-teller at a school carnival.

The same man was in the grocery store and Andrea found herself watching him, moving her cart slowly down one aisle after another, looking at boxes of cereal and pretending great interest in their contents, while actually watching him. He was a huge man, probably the biggest man she had ever seen in her life. At her height she never had to look up to men. Not only was he very tall, he was—big. Broad shoulders stretched the knit fabric of his shirt across muscles that rippled when he reached for his package. The immense shoulders tapered down to a relatively small waist and hips. All the proportions were right, it was just that everything about him seemed larger than life. When he rounded the corner, she hastily threw her usual selections into the cart and quickly followed him to the next aisle.

Andrea's food choices were as eclectic as her dress. She ate when she was hungry, whenever that happened to be, and because of that, rarely took the time to cook full meals. Eating was a necessity, a necessity that interrupted her other activities, and usually it only took her about thirty minutes to breeze through the store.

Today she extended that thirty minutes, watching the man select his vegetables or choose enough meat to feed a football team. Scanning the meat counter while he checked his list she suddenly knew what she wanted. Her favorite meal. The one she only ate when she was alone, liver smothered in onions and spinach. For the first time in weeks she felt really hungry. Her attention shifted, now on the liver waiting for her expert treatment, and she quickly finished her shopping.

But her concentration on gathering groceries proved brief when she found herself in the same checkout line with him. Again she studied him while pretending to leaf through a magazine. He kept his back to her presenting, at most, a one-quarter view, and seemed unaware of her presence. Only when his groceries were being bagged did he turn.

"Am I mistaken, or are you following me?"

"You must be mistaken." She practically stammered in her embarrassment at being caught doing just that. If her voice didn't give her away, her face would, she thought, feeling it turn several shades of pink. She wasn't one to follow a man around the grocery store. In fact, she rarely paid much attention to men at all, and certainly never in such an incidental setting.

"Too bad. I thought maybe you would tell my fortune, read tea leaves, whatever."

"Friday is my day off."

In the drugstore she had been aware of dark brown eyes, but these weren't just dark brown. They were a liquid brown filled with sparks of life, little golden flecks lighting the darkness like sunshine through thick trees. His hair was thick and straight, not the hint of a curl or wave as it fell over a broad forehead. He had strong high, cheekbones emphasized by a sleek, dark beard, so carefully trimmed that it looked as smooth as satin.

His groceries were bagged and he turned without another word. Andrea watched his long strides as he pushed the overflowing cart from the store and wondered absently if all that food was for him alone, or if he was married and had a family.

Driving home, she couldn't seem to stop thinking about the stranger. Goodness, he had been tall. And not just tall, either; huge. She was five foot ten, so he must have been at least six and a half feet tall for her to have to look up like that. What would it be like to kiss someone that tall? To have to really look up to be kissed—as in the movies, him bending down, she reaching up, head tilted back, spine arched to meet the curve of his bending torso. He had had a beautiful mouth. Firm, well-defined lips set off by that smooth, black beard.

"Andrea MacLarson, I do believe you're cracking up. One look at an unusual man and you start imagining love scenes. He hardly looked at you other than to laugh."

Andrea was surprised at the path her mind had taken. She had never been the type who sat around thinking about a stranger she saw or imagining scenarios that included kissing. She had never been the type who fantasized about men at all. What was wrong with her today?

"Probably nothing unusual," she muttered as she steered the car around the last few narrow curves to the small house. Her mother had always said idleness was dangerous, and if her thoughts weren't proof of that, then she didn't know what would be.

Once home, Andrea dumped the groceries and packages onto the kitchen table, fed the cats, and prepared the liver and spinach. Pushing the still-unpacked groceries and packages aside to make room for her plate, she began reading one of the romance novels she had bought.

Only after thoroughly enjoying each morsel of food and two chapters of the book did she put the plate into the sink and run some water over it. Turning, she glanced around the small, cluttered rooms.

The living area was divided into two halves separated by a fireplace and a railing. The right half was three steps higher than the left and served as the bedroom. An old iron bed, whose springs protested at any move was placed directly behind the chimney. An old dresser with a dull mirror served as the only storage for clothes other than several large pegs along the back wall.

Large, multipaned windows overlooked the town nestled snugly in the valley below. An old sofa whose cushions were forever misshapen sat under one of the windows. A scarred coffee table, an old rocker that creaked comfortably and a rickety bookshelf filled to overflowing with books and magazines completed the furnishings.

There was no division between the living room and kitchen. Exposed to any who entered—which so far had only been herself and Mr. Andrews—were the old appliances, a stained and chipped enamel sink and cupboards without doors. Even the pipes beneath the sink were not enclosed.

Someone in the past had finally conceded to modernization by enclosing half the back porch and installing indoor plumbing that was reached by going out the back door to the porch and then into the bathroom. She had decided it was better than bathing in the large tin tub that was propped against the back of the house, but not much.

Andrea turned and stared out the wide windows as the questions settled around her once more. She had spent a long time that morning being introspective and she didn't want to think now. All the thinking in the world would never explain why Susie had left her this house, with the crazy stipulation that she stay here for a month before she made a decision about what to do with it. Once she had spent the prescribed time, she was free to do whatever she wished with the place.

She could have tolerated the house if she had had something to do, but Susie had also stipulated that she was not to bring work of any type. As a result, after only two days she was already going crazy, imagining things like kissing a total stranger.

Andrea turned away from the window. This house didn't fit into her real life in any way. She had responsibilities and obligations. What in the world was she supposed to do for another twenty-eight days? Maybe there was a crisis at the office and she could go home. Crossing her fingers, she picked up the phone and dialed.

"MacLarson and Costley, Julie Costley speaking."

"Hi, Julie."

"Andrea. I didn't expect you to call today."

"I've called every day," Andrea reminded her. Nothing in the will had said she couldn't make a phone call and at least keep tabs on things.

"Time difference, boss." Julie laughed.

Andrea glanced around. No clocks were in sight, and she wasn't at all sure what time it was. She couldn't even remember where she had put her watch. She had been here two days and already she was losing track of things.

"I'm sorry. I guess the day just got away from me."

"I'm glad to hear you finally did something other than chew your fingernails and call me," Julie said. "So, what exciting things have you been up to?"

Andrea grimaced. She couldn't tell Julie she had sat on the front steps for hours, moping about being stuck here. Well, it had started out as moping, but had quickly turned into just sitting and enjoying the view. And she would never admit to following the proverbial tall, dark and handsome stranger around the grocery store. "Just some shopping. How late is it?"

"Almost five here."

Andrea knew Julie well. Not only were they business partners, they had been close friends for years. "You must have a big weekend planned to sound so anxious about the time."

"David's made reservations for dinner and said dress to the hilt."

"What's up?"

"I don't know. He may have closed that deal he's been working on for so long, the one on the Chattahoochee, or it may be..." Julie's voice trailed off dreamily.

"You think he might pop the question?" Julie had been dating David for several months and made no secret of the fact that she was ready for the relationship to progress.

"I don't know for sure." A small sigh filtered across the wire. "You know which one don't you?"

"I'll keep my fingers crossed if you want me to."

"That's a true friend." Julie laughed again. "If I want you to. We're talking about my future!"

"I know, but if you want to mess it up with marriage, I'm behind you all the way," Andrea teased.

"You know me," Julie said. "I want it all."

"You have the best of everything now. A career you love, your own condo and a steady romance. You're going to upset a well-balanced life."

Julie laughed once more, well aware of Andrea's reluctance to make commitments in her personal life. "It's called settling down."

"Better you than me." Andrea had always assumed that someday marriage would be a part of her life, too. It did seem to just happen, eventually. But it sounded so restrictive—so many demands to be met for so many people. There were enough demands in life as it was, without adding all the frustrations of meshing one schedule to another.

"I can't see myself keeping house," Andrea mused, her gaze darting about the messy rooms. The thought of the stranger's overly filled shopping cart added another dreaded idea. "Or cooking three times a day."

"Someday, Andrea, you are going to fall head over heels in love and not care if all you do the rest of your life is cook."

"My mother wishes." Andrea laughed. Tina MacLarson was perfectly comfortable with her daughter's choice to stay single and concentrate on her career; she even encouraged it. Andrea propped her feet on the cluttered coffee table. "So, how is everything at the office?"

"Everything is fine, Andrea. Why don't you just relax and enjoy your time off? I'll bet you haven't even played tourist yet."

"No, not yet," Andrea admitted reluctantly. "But—"

"No buts," Julie interrupted. "See the sites and relax. Just enjoy yourself while you decide what you want to do with the house."

"I could decide at home, now that I've seen the place."

Julie knew the stipulations as well as she did. They had discussed them at length, and neither of them had come up with a reasonable explanation for Susie's strange demand.

"You can't make a reasonable decision without seeing the area. Just have some fun. Speaking of which, I need to get out of here and soak in some yummy bubbles."

"David doesn't have a chance," Andrea told her friend.

"That's the general idea," Julie said. "You can spend part of your leisure imaging the beautiful, sexy business partner having dinner in a candle-lit restaurant with a gorgeous hunk of male."

"I might just do that. You'll have to let me know what happens."

"You'll be one of the first."

Andrea shook her head as she replaced the phone. She could picture the scene Julie had mentioned, but the face she saw shadowed with soft, flickering light wasn't David's; it was the stranger's, the dark eyes reflecting tiny flames of light.

"This is absolutely ridiculous," she muttered as she stood up. She had seen a man, he had asked her a silly question, and now she couldn't stop thinking about him. She was going to go crazy if she didn't find something to do for the next few weeks.

She had to get busy. Now! But busy doing what? she wondered as she glanced again around the cluttered rooms. She didn't feel like sitting inside, and she didn't have anything to do other than read a book or go out and play tourist, and it was too late to do that. She could visit Mr. Andrews. At least she would get some exercise in the process.

The late-fall afternoon was warm. Mr. Andrews's house was eight miles by the road, but only two if she walked through the woods. She started through the trees, following a well-worn path to the first field, through the stubble of hay and on into the next stretch of trees.

The attorney had given her William Andrews's name. He had acted as caretaker of the house. He had been the one who had arranged to have the house aired and cleaned before she arrived. It seemed strange that he had not been able to—or would not—answer any of her questions about her aunt. He claimed he had never met her.

Bill Andrews was a typical mountain man of average height, with sharp, blue eyes that missed very little. His skin was weathered from years spent working outdoors, and he always had a plug of tobacco in his mouth. That habit Andrea found slightly revolting.

But then, he had already decided that her poor housekeeping skills were the reason she was an old maid. Thirty—an old maid! His view of the world hadn't changed with the times. He still thought women should be married, stay home and have children. "Do what God put them here to do," he had said. She had made the mistake of asking what God's plan for men was, and had been told in no uncertain terms that it was to protect and provide for women.

He also didn't think it was proper for her to be living alone so far from town and with no family to protect her. He hadn't liked it at all when she arrived alone. Despite his initial reluctance to accept her living arrangements, they were developing a warm friendship. It was an honest relationship. Each of them felt free to speak their mind.

Seated on his back porch with a glass of iced tea, Andrea looked forward to the gossip Mr. Andrews always shared. She had hardly gotten settled in the straight-backed chair before he imparted a piece of news that set her heart beating a little too fast.

"By the way, you got a new neighbor."

"Really? Who?"

"Name's Bart Collins. Hear tell he's a giant of a fella, nearly seven feet tall and three hundred pounds. But you know how things like that go. You should hear some of the things I've heard about you."

Andrea caught the teasing twinkle in his blue eyes and grinned. "That I read tea leaves and ride a broom." She was still dressed in her gypsy clothes.

Mr. Andrews laughed. "Ain't heard that one yet, missy."

"So where is this Bart Collins living?" Bart Collins. She liked the sound of it. The name fitted the man.

"At the old Smith place."

The old Smith place was closer to Bill Andrews than to her. She had never been down the small side road where the house was, nor had she hiked in that area yet. But the Smith place was the nearest house, so it did make him a neighbor. "Did he buy it?" She had also been told by a real estate agent that the house was never rented.

"Don't think so. Ain't heard nothin' 'bout it in town. Why?"

She wanted to know if people were interested in buying property on this side of the valley. Angel Fire, with its condominiums, ski lifts and exquisite houses, was on the side opposite her aunt's house.

"Just curious," she said with a shrug.

"If you're curious you could go out to dinner. Bound to bump into him that way."

There weren't that many restaurants in the area, especially during the off-season. "With all the food he bought, he won't be going out to eat," Andrea muttered. "His wife will be cooking all day long."

Mr. Andrews settled back in his chair. "My Martha always felt proud of her cookin'. 'Course, she wanted a day off now 'n' then, like anybody else. Used to take her out or cook myself."

Andrea stared at the older man, trying to picture him cooking dinner for his wife. She couldn't quite imagine him either wearing an apron or as a man with a liberated marriage.

"Marriage is a partnership, missy."

Maybe. Maybe it was sometimes, but usually it seemed that all the responsibility fell onto the woman's shoulders. It was up to the woman to see to the house, the children, the food—and usually to work, too.

"Now, if this Bart Collins bought all that food, maybe he'll be cookin' you dinner."

"Cook for me?"

"He ain't married. Ain't that what you been wanting to ow?"

She couldn't think of a thing to say, and she didn't care to tangle with the mischievous twinkle in the older man's eyes.

Andrea woke before sunrise. The book she had been reading was under her cheek, serving as a pillow. The cats were curled on her, Thoth in the small of her back and Mercury nestled in the crook of her knee. An old rerun of *Gunsmoke* was on the television set she had never turned off the night before.

Though half-asleep, she was already restless. She was used to being busy. She was used to having things to do, a business to take care of, family to worry about. Susie had known how much she hated being idle. It wasn't fair of her aunt to ask her to do something like this, to waste an entire month of her life.

Already irritated with the day, she headed for the kitchen to start some coffee. But the drink only made her feel more restless. Knowing she had to get out of the house or scream, she returned to the bedroom and dressed in the first garments she found.

The sun was barely over the horizon when she left the house. Beneath the trees it was still dark and dusky. She paused to watch a deer sniff nervously and then leap into the trees again, before she continued toward the outcrop of rock she had found the first day. Once there she climbed down and curled up in the warmth of the early-morning sun, wondering how she would survive a month with nothing to do but read or go sight-seeing.

Her outcrop overlooked the valley and town below. The sun climbed into the sky, lighting each new piece of world. It was a spot meant for daydreaming, but Andrea had never allowed herself to indulge in that pastime, well, not since she was a teenager. When she realized that her mind kept drifting, she decided it was time to leave.

A movement caught her eye as she started to rise and she stood still, waiting. Two dogs ran from the trees below into a natural clearing, and then the man appeared. She settled down again and watched. He walked with long, purposeful strides across the clearing, the dogs running before him. All too quickly the trio disappeared into the trees.

Andrea sighed as she closed her eyes, thinking about his eyes and the beard. Jim had had a mustache that tickled at the wrong times, but she had never kissed a man with a beard. And his mouth had looked very sensual. Firm, well-defined lips, the bottom one slightly fuller, the kind of lips... *Whoever or whatever Bart Collins is, you won't be kissing him. You've definitely gone crazy.* Shaking her head, she rose to go, only to be met with a low, rumbling growl.

Two large golden retrievers stood guard, one on either side of the rock she was perched on, each waiting for her to make a move. *Great. The man isn't big enough. He has to bring along an army to protect him against deer and squirrel.* Feeling very vulnerable, her exposed throat level with their fangs, she looked from one dog to the other and slowly sat down again. "Good dog," she said weakly. "Go home." The only response was another low, rumbling growl.

Bart strode through the forest. The tension that had bound his muscles for months didn't seem to lessen, even with the activity. He had always stayed in shape, and the few miles he had walked hadn't even caused his heart rate to increase.

Forcefully he pushed the gloomy thoughts aside. Justin had been kind enough to offer the house, to give him a place to be away from everything. He should at least put it to the purpose for which it had been meant. He had wanted peace and quiet and time. He had them. But as usual he was being impatient, expecting the change of scenery to instantly transform everything.

The dogs dashed ahead in the trees, their fur glinting for a moment in the early-morning sun as they followed an unseen trail and headed uphill to his left. They bounded along, more eager, happier with the world than he. Their world was filled with intriguing scents, full stomachs and friendly, affectionate rubs. His was full of greed and acrimony, bitterness and broken dreams.

If he were a dog he could find happiness in the trail of a rabbit or the warmth of the sun on his back. He was a man, though, and what he saw was land that could bring a fortune if it was developed, and bitterness between friends and family. Bart lengthened his step to a run as the dogs growled. Damn Justin for training them like that. Some innocent hiker was probably looking for the nearest tree.

Bart reached the top of the ridge, barely noticing the spectacular view. What held his attention was the woman sitting on a rock ledge, staring wide-eyed at the two dogs. "Red! Brandy! Back!" The dogs moved back and sat down, quiet but alert. He would send those two back with Justin this weekend. He needed solitude, not a lawsuit caused by two four-footed friends.

Andrea looked up at the towering figure standing above her. Her eyes ran from the expensive, leather hiking boots to the tightly fitted jeans that strained over his thighs, and slowly up his massive chest to his face. Everything he wore was obviously new. He could have stepped off the page of a catalog.

He looked exactly like she felt, someone on a vacation they had no idea what to do with. The only difference was that he had obviously planned this himself and bought the appropriate clothes. But the people she had seen camping or fishing had been wearing clothes that had been obviously worn and exposed to the rigors of the outdoors. They looked at home standing by a stream or sitting on a log.

Rather than extend his hand to help the woman off the rock, Bart sighed inwardly as he saw her wide, green eyes travel slowly from his feet to his face. Now she was probably more afraid of him than she had been of the dogs. It had taken him years to learn how to handle the challenges that his imposing physique presented. There was always someone who wanted to prove his size meant nothing. Women, on the other hand, were both intrigued and frightened.

"I'm sorry. Did the dogs hurt you?"

"No. They just startled me." Her shoulders straightened slightly. "You really shouldn't let them run free if they are trained to attack. Lots of people hike around here."

He resisted the urge to smile at her reprimand. If she was afraid, she wasn't going to let him see it, though there was a hint of uncertainty in her voice. "I'll remember. Sorry to have bothered you."

He turned to leave and she couldn't help watching the play of hard muscle beneath his jeans as he lifted one leg to step onto the trail. His clothes might be new, but he was obviously in good condition. He turned back, catching her gaze. Andrea stood and needlessly brushed off her jeans, avoiding his eyes—and hopefully hiding the blush that she knew stained her cheeks.

"Excuse me, but have we met before?" Again she looked up, only now her wide, green eyes were shadowed with thoughts he couldn't read.

Did she really look that different? No, she just hadn't made the impression on him that he had on her. "Yes, yesterday."

Bart sat down on a rock near her. He knew exactly who she was, the gypsy fortune-teller who had trailed him through the grocery store. He couldn't have forgotten those wide, green eyes or those long, slender legs if he had tried. And he had tried. She was tall and svelte, with small breasts and hips, yet she had an aura of femininity that didn't need voluptuousness to hold a man's eye. Even the way she was dressed today, in worn jeans and a man's shirt, couldn't hide the feminine appeal.

"I'm sorry. I can't place you." Though he hadn't forgotten, he didn't want to encourage her, either.

"I'm the gypsy fortune-teller."

Her hair had been tied back beneath a black scarf, hiding the rich, warm, coppery shade of auburn. Even now he couldn't be sure of its length. It was loosely twisted in one thick braid. He hadn't realized how slender she was beneath that full skirt and loose blouse. She had also had on makeup that hid the dusting of freckles across her nose.

"And you are Bart Collins."

Bart tensed at the unexpected statement. One reason he had accepted Justin's offer of the house was because he didn't want to be known, he had wanted to be anonymous. "How do you know who I am?" he asked, when he really wanted to know how much she knew about who he was.

She smiled. "Gypsy fortune-tellers know these things."

"You asked in town."

A name would be easily available in a small town. Justin had said he would have to tell the old man who kept an eye on the house, and of course he had probably told the woman who had come in and opened the house. He had forgotten how quickly information could be passed. He was fairly certain Justin wouldn't have said anything, but not certain his identity wasn't known. His face had been plastered across tabloids and newspapers on the East Coast for weeks.

"Not at all. I saw it in my crystal ball. You're staying at the old Smith place."

There was a mixture of honesty and teasing in the statement. Curious as to what the local gossip was, he asked, "And what else did you see in your crystal ball?"

Since that was all Mr. Andrews had known, it was all she had seen. "It's against our code of ethics to look further than that without permission."

"You have my permission to look anytime you please," he said, laughing.

Andrea wondered if his permission to look included staring at him. She knew she was, but couldn't seem to stop. She watched the play of light in his straight, black hair, then the way his shirt outlined his shoulders when he rested his elbows on his knees, and the way his thighs stretched the denim tightly. Andrea tried to shake off the silly thoughts. He had sat down just a few feet from her and she hesitated to leave, unsure why she was staying. He certainly wasn't paying any attention to her. His eyes, however, were drinking in the view of the valley and the mountains beyond, drinking in the shadings of gold and purple.

"It's a beautiful spot. Do you come here often?"

"It is beautiful, isn't it?" she agreed, turning to look over the wide valley to the mountains beyond. "It's the perfect place to sit and think."

"What do gypsies think about?"

She wondered how she could manage to sound mysterious and all-knowing when she looked like a tomboy. "Many things." Recently too many things had been connected with this man. Too many times she had thought about his size, his sparkling eyes or his deep, resonant voice.

"Do you read palms or just crystal balls and tea leaves?"

She turned and looked up at the unexpected question. His eyes were dancing with light, and one corner of his mouth was quirked into a half smile. "Oh, definitely palms, of course. They are much more accurate than the other methods."

"You probably also practice making love potions. A little witchcraft on the side, but all for the good of mankind."

She smiled, enjoying the teasing. "I see you were asking about me in town."

"Just a lucky guess."

"Very lucky then," she said, lifting her chin. "My reputation is well-known."

"Would you read my palm?"

# Two

Andrea stared at the upturned palm that had been extended with the question. Now what was she supposed to say? "These things are best done when the inner powers are in tune."

"Friday is your day off and Saturday your powers are out of tune." His eyes twinkled and his beard glinted blue-black in the morning sun. "Your reputation is probably based on hearsay rather than results."

She couldn't ignore the teasing challenge in his voice or the laughter in his eyes. She climbed the few feet that separated them and stopped in front of him, her own palm extended. When he looked up, one brow raised questioningly, she smiled and said, "You must always cross the palm with silver."

Chuckling that same soft rumble of sound she had heard in the drugstore, he reached into his pocket, pulled out some change and dropped it into her open hand. The coins were warm against her skin, warm and alive from the heat of his body. She stared at them, not sure why they felt that way.

"Not enough?"

"Oh, no, it's fine."

Now what was she going to say? His eyes were dancing and sparkling with fun at their silliness. Maybe it didn't matter what she said. For a moment she let herself wonder how it would feel to be held in those powerful arms, to be pulled against that massive chest. Frightening, she decided quickly. He was just too big. A person could get lost in his arms. But his hand was waiting and she reached for it.

The contact was electric. Her hand tingled at the touch and she almost pulled it away. Her mind went totally blank, aware only of the strange sensation as she stared into the upturned palm. His hand completely hid hers. It was very large and well formed, the fingers long, the palm wide but not fleshy. His hand was firm and strong, but not rough or calloused. Like his clothes, it suggested a life spent in offices and health clubs.

"What do you see?" he asked, breaking into her thoughts.

She traced a line on his palm, the warmth singeing the tip of her finger. "You will live a long and happy life free from worry and care. Fortune will come easily to you." Bitter laughter interrupted her and she looked up.

She wasn't sure what she had said to cause his reaction. It didn't matter. The pain was there, openly displayed in velvet-brown eyes fringed with short, dark lashes. Suddenly it was very important to banish the pain from his life. "We are talking of the future, Mr. Collins, not the past. The past is finished." Something changed in his expression, now it had a softening, almost wistful look.

"So, tell me of the future, Gypsy."

She tore her eyes from his and looked back at the palm of his hand, a hand dwarfing her own. What do I say? she wondered, absently tracing a line. "Your secret hopes and dreams will be fulfilled. You will accomplish what you came here to do. You will be successful and famous." She glanced up through her lashes. "Didn't he want fame? "Yet the fame will be on your terms." Now his eyes softened again.

What did he want to hear? Who or what had hurt him that much?

Lightly she traced another line. Never had she touched someone and felt burned—burned by a sweet sensation she now experienced. And never had she stood holding a man's hand, perfectly content to do nothing more than that for the entire day.

"And love? Will there be a great love in my life, Witch?"

She almost giggled at the question. "Yes. You will have a very great romance. Thousands of women will dream of you as their lover." Probably every woman who had ever met him had. "But only one will have your attention."

"And this one, Gypsy? Tell me of this one."

"That had not been revealed yet," she countered with a frown. "It will come clear in its own time."

He slowly withdrew his hand from hers, dragging the back of it across her palm in such a way that a numbing tingle raced the length of her arm to her shoulder, taking her breath with it.

"I think it has already been made clear."

His eyes were teasing, but the statement turned on alarm bells throughout her body. She knew she was reacting to him on a purely physical level, and she didn't like the fact to be so evident that he could comment on it. She certainly didn't want him to think she would act on her feelings.

"What is your name, Gypsy?"

She wasn't going to complicate this situation further. "Gypsies consider their names secret and personal," she said and started to move away, feeling totally shaken by the undercurrents that flowed around her.

He caught her hand, stopping her. "Why?"

"Tradition." She looked at the hand holding hers, totally engulfing her own slender one. "Tradition states that knowing a name gives you power over a person." And he did have some kind of power over her. She felt caught in a spell.

"Are you afraid of me?"

"No." No, she wasn't afraid of him. She was terrified.

Andrea wasn't naive, but she wasn't really experienced, either. Except for one rather brief love affair in college, she had kept all her relationships casual. Nothing in her past had led her to expect anything like this. It was stunning. It was enchanting. It was drugging and addictive. She had never reacted to anyone this way, caught in a web of entice- ment when nothing had really happened. His eyes traveled slowly over her and she fought the urge to look down and make sure everything was properly buttoned and covered. At last his eyes came back to her face.

"You're very beautiful, Gypsy."

Andrea swallowed nervously. She wasn't beautiful. She was too thin, had no figure and had too many freckles. He studied her face for a long moment. "Very beautiful." Her hand was still caught in his. His fingers curled around it with the lightest of touches, yet she felt incapable of breaking the contact.

"Why are you trembling?"

She couldn't explain why she was trembling. Well, she could have, but she wasn't about to try. And no simple, in- consequential answers came to her mind, a mind that was rapidly going completely blank.

"Don't be frightened."

Andrea was sure her trembling was not from fear of him. It was her reaction to him that was making her tremble, de- spite her best efforts not to. It was the warmth of his hand on hers and the way his eyes held hers in an unrelenting, yet seductive gaze. Or it might have been the texture of his voice as it floated in the still, morning air. He had a distinctive voice, deep but not rough, gentle yet very masculine.

No, this intangible thing wasn't fear. It was a tension that had increased her pulse and used up all the oxygen in the atmosphere, making it hard to breath easily. The air tin- gled with the power of an impending storm, yet the sky re- mained clear and crystal blue. The world around her seemed uneffected by the forces encapsulating her, surrounding her and making the air shimmer between them.

"I'm not afraid," she lied. She needed to break the contact, change the tone. "Are people often frightened around you?"

Bart tensed, then realized she was teasing him. There was a sparkle in her eyes, almost daring him to confess all his sins. "Only in dark alleys and empty hallways."

Andrea understood. She imagined herself alone, in a city; she would be startled, even frightened if he appeared unexpectedly in a dark place. It was only human nature to be frightened of something bigger and stronger than oneself. But here, in the bright light of morning, in this tranquil setting, she could see the gentleness behind the size, the sensitivity behind the strength. She had nothing to fear from this man, at least physically.

Bart looked down at the slender hand still resting in his. She was strikingly beautiful. Tall, slender and so vibrantly alive. The life poured from her hand to his, from her eyes to his, an energy and awareness that filled the air like a living force. There was a timeless quality about her. And her eyes radiated an understanding that went deeper than spoken words.

No, she wasn't frightened, but she was aware. Just as aware as he was. He couldn't help wondering how she would react if he took her into his arms. She trembled at his touch. He could almost feel the tremors that would course through her when he held her. He could almost taste her sweet mouth. It would be warm and pliant at first, curious, testing. The curiosity for both of them would quickly change to fire.

Bart stood slowly, releasing her hand even more slowly. He touched her cheek, allowing himself to satisfy that little bit of curiosity. As he had known it would be, her skin was like warm satin.

"I have to go, Gypsy." He snapped his fingers for the dogs' attention and without looking back, left. He had not come here to get tangled up with anyone, no matter how enchanting the little witch happened to be. The very last thing he wanted in the world was involvement.

Andrea stood still, hardly breathing, long after Bart had disappeared from sight. Feeling dazed and stunned, as if she had come into contact with a live electric wire, she finally left, slipping through the woods by a roundabout route before picking up her path and returning to the small house.

Totally shaken by the experience, she decided that she had to find something to fill the hours and keep her mind active. If nothing else, she would spend her time sight-seeing. Idleness was a definite hazard to mental health and sanity.

By the time she had changed into a presentable pair of jeans and a bright, cotton sweater, she had almost convinced herself that she had imagined more than half her reaction. She didn't believe people responded on a level like that. There was no such thing as an instant awareness or understanding. There was no such thing as an instant attraction, either. Her imagination had simply been running away with her.

Andrea tossed her purse in the general direction of the sofa, kicked her shoes in the direction of the bed and sank onto the steps. Dirty cups and glasses were scattered around the entire house. An empty cottage cheese container, a plate with dried crumbs, and miscellaneous items scattered about showed how little attention she had paid to the house or her meals in the last few days. She scooped up an arm load of dishes and trash and took it to the kitchen, leaving it in a heap on the already cluttered counter.

Looking around the small house from the bedroom to the kitchen, she shook her head. She had always lived as she wanted within her own four walls. It was her one spot of rebellion. If she didn't want to dust or sweep she didn't, and obviously it had been a long time since she had cared to do very much at all with the house. She didn't care to now, either. She needed a break.

Muttering angrily to herself, she collected a towel and robe. She needed a break from her "vacation." She needed a break from trying to fill empty hours. She had spent the last few days sight-seeing. There was a surprising amount to see in the area, everything from Mount Capulin, an extinct

volcano, to art galleries and museums. Every time she had
talked to someone, they had asked if she had seen something else. Her list of things to do was growing more rapidly than she would have imagined. But she was no less
bored and no less frustrated with her situation than she had
been before.

After showering and shampooing her hair, she stood in
front of the dresser. Nothing appealed to her today. Finally
she pulled on a pair of jeans and a loose-fitting, cotton top,
reminding herself she had to do some laundry. She slipped
her feet into her jogging shoes and brushed her still-damp
hair, leaving it lying loose about her shoulders. The sun
would dry it soon enough and she now had a purpose for her
walk. The water heater was on the blink again. Mr. Andrews would at least know whom she could get to fix it.

The afternoon was warm and her hair dried quickly as she
walked. Mr. Andrews was working in his garden when she
arrived almost an hour later, hot and flushed from the hike.
He looked up and waved as she crossed the last field of
stubble.

"How's the garden?" she asked.

"Finished for the year." Mr. Andrews gave her a
thoughtful look. "That Mr. Collins fella has been asking
round about you." He spat a brown stream into the dirt near
his feet. "'Cepting no one knew who he was a-talkin'
about."

Andrea's heart did a funny little skip. "What did he say?"
And when and where and why? Somewhere deep inside she
was shocked at how pleased she was that he had been in-
quiring.

"Was down to the hardware store yesterday. This fella,
and he is a giant of a man, them stories ain't far off on that
account." He glanced at her, his eyes sparkling. "But you
know that, don't you."

It wasn't really a question, and Andrea saw no reason to
deny the obvious. She nodded.

"Well, he was buying an ax and a saw. Must be plannin'
to cut his own firewood." He paused to straighten his back
and look at the sky with a practiced eye. "Won't be long

afore we need some wood of an evening, either." He looked around the garden. "Want some coffee, missy?"

"That would be nice."

The old goat was going to make her squirm. He knew he had her curiosity piqued, and now he would drag this out endlessly. She followed him to the back porch and sat down on the straight chair he indicated. A wide shelf ran along the length of the porch, and at one point an enamel pan and mirror hung from pegs on one of the posts. She wondered, not for the first time, if he shaved out here in the morning.

"Here ya go," he said, setting two stoneware mugs down.

Andrea smiled and sipped the scalding brew, knowing the liquid would be thick as syrup.

"Now, where was I? Oh yes, well, anyways, let's see. Zeke and Hal was there and we was sitting talkin' about winter. Going to be a rough one this year. All the signs indicate it." She nodded her head impatiently. Again he surveyed the sky, sniffing the air as if he were in direct communication with Mother Nature. "It's goin' to be a bad winter this year, for sure."

Andrea knew the older man was aware how much she wanted to shake the information about Bart Collins out of him, so instead, she tried to go along. "I imagine it's very beautiful here during the winter. The view from my house must be spectacular." She was unaware of the wistful note in her voice or the way her eyes drank in the mountains and the beauty surrounding them.

"Well, you'll be much better off if you don't see it from up there. Get stuck with no electricity and phone down. Ain't no way for a young woman alone to be a-livin'."

She gave in. "So what happened at the hardware store, Mr. Andrews?"

His eyes glinted joyfully at her question. "Well now, we was just sittin' round, talking 'bout the weather and some such, and in walks this man. I don't pay much attention to gossip, mind you, but I swear that's the biggest man I ever saw. Ain't no person alive would want to tangle with that man."

Andrea nodded thoughtfully. He was big, yet she hadn't been afraid of him. He had seemed so gentle. Maybe it was the quiet way he spoke and moved or possibly it was the teasing laughter in his eyes, but nothing about him had indicated anything but gentleness.

"Anyhow, he starts heftin' axes in his hand and such. Young Dave Benson asks can he help him. He says no thank you, and so Dave steps away and just watches, as we all was a-doin'."

She could picture the way silence would have fallen over the group when he entered.

"Anyway, this Mr. Collins, he finally takes the heaviest ax and then picks a saw and takes them to the cash register." He took a long drink of the coffee and then looked at Andrea. "Care for more?"

"Oh, no, thank you."

"Well, think I'll have another cup."

He got up and went back into the house, and Andrea had to fight the urge to follow him and demand he finish the story. But that was just what he wanted. At last he came back, sat down in his straight-backed chair, and after sending another brown stream over the side of the porch, continued.

"Well, Young Dave asks him if there's anything else, and he says as how there isn't at the moment. All very polite and proper and then he says, 'I understand there's a gypsy living around here.' Well, we all look at each other and ol' Zeke, he taps his temple. Young Dave frowns and shakes his head. Says he doesn't know of any, and then this Mr. Collins says, 'Well, maybe she's a witch. She reads palms and tea leaves.'

"Well, then a-course I knowed he was talkin' about you, missy, 'cause last Friday you said something about readin' tea leaves. But I was havin' too much fun watching Zeke roll his eyes and Hal choke on his chew to put things to rights." Mr. Andrews would never admit he was protecting her by his silence. "So Young Dave shakes his head and looks at the ax, and you can see he thinks maybe this man ain't really safe to be sellin' these things to. So he tells him no, hadn't heard of any witches, or fortune-tellers, either. Well,'' Bill Andrews continued after a long chuckle and another gulp of coffee, "Dave allows as how someone must 'a' been pullin' his leg, but this Mr. Collins shakes his head."

By now it was taking all of Andrea's willpower not to burst into laughter. She shook her head at the inexplicable behavior of the stranger and took a drink of the thick mud in her cup. It had the desired effect of killing all thought of laughter. She hadn't thought Bart Collins would ask about her, especially not in places as public as the hardware store, for all ears to hear. This story was probably all over the town. The poor man. Rumor probably had it that they had a madman in their midst.

"So, this Mr. Collins, he looks thoughtful for a moment, picks up his tools and says, more to hisself than us, 'I saw her the other morning. She read my palm.' Well, missy, he stood there a-lookin' at his right hand like it was somethin' magical. Then he shrugs and walks out."

Andrea rubbed her left hand nervously against the side of the mug. "And that's all?"

"'Nough, ain't it? Thinks you're some kind of a witch." He frowned slightly. "Missy, you shouldn't be talkin' to strange men and pretendin' such like. Folk don't understand 'bout witches." He watched her for a moment, a grin twitching at the corner of his mouth. "So what did ya tell him?"

Andrea laughed then. He wasn't really upset after all, just cautioning her. "Just that all his dreams would come true, that he would be rich and famous and find a wonderful woman to love him."

Mr. Andrews looked thoughtful for a moment. "Maybe he will, maybe he will, at that." He grinned and settled back in his chair. "At least that last part." Mischievous blue eyes flicked in her direction and then back to the mountains.

Andrea wasn't one to back down quickly. She pretended to consider the idea for a moment, took a sip of the cool coffee, then spoke. "I think he has a much greater chance at the fame and fortune. I'd guess him to be in his mid-thirties, and there aren't many single women in this town between the ages of thirty and forty.''

Angel Fire was a ski resort community. Its year-round population was only about four hundred people, and most of those were either stable families who had businesses connected with the resort or older people, like Mr. Andrews, who had lived in the area before the ski slopes had been built.

Mr. Andrews agreed with a meaningful look. "Girls round here either get married or move away. Six years ain't a bad age difference. I was ten years older than my Martha.''

Andrea didn't like the direction of the conversation now at all. "Thank you for the coffee. I'd better start back if I don't want to be out after dark.''

Bill Andrews really got upset whenever he learned she was out in the woods alone at night. She knew the rugged mountains were hazardous, especially at night. Even people who knew the area well were known to get lost or fall in the dark forests. She rarely walked anywhere other than along the gentle path to her rock after sunset.

Mr. Andrews looked up at the sky. "Yeah, winter's a-comin' early this year. Be nice to have a young man around during long cold evenings. Two can stay a lot warmer than one in cold weather.''

Ignoring his comment, she got around to the purpose of her visit. "Speaking of warm, the hot-water heater isn't working right. Who can I call to look at it?''

"Old thing's probably just wearin' out. I'll be happy to come up tomorrow and take a look at it for you.''

"Does the fireplace work?'' It would be nice to sit in front of a fire when the evenings get cooler.

"Should if the chimney ain't blocked. Ain't been used in a lot of years. I'll bring along some wood tomorrow and take a peek up her.'' He chuckled and tilted his chair back. "Sittin' in front of fires together is real nice, too.''

Andrea paused and looked at the older man. Bill Andrews definitely had a romantic streak a mile wide, she decided, and it was best to nip such ideas in the bud.

"Mr. Andrews, I'm not interested in Bart Collins and he isn't interested in me." The first part of the statement was more of a fervent wish, and she wasn't sure what the second part was.

"A man don't risk makin' a fool a' hisself when he ain't interested, missy."

And then again, sometimes the better part of valor was silence. "I'd better be going."

"Nice home-cooked dinner and sittin' in front of a fire sure sounds good, don't it, missy."

It wasn't a question, and Andrea would never have admitted that it did indeed sound good. With a smile she left.

She really wasn't interested in Bart Collins. Just because she had thought of him constantly the last few days meant nothing. Just because she had found herself looking for him as she walked through Taos or stood in a gallery didn't mean she was interested. Just because she had spent as much time studying the visitors' register in the museum in Cimarron as the displays—to see if he had been there—didn't mean she was interested in him.

Just because she could still feel the warmth of his hand on hers or remember the charged air between them that had left her breathless, it didn't mean she was interested. What it meant was that she was sensible enough to avoid the man and the temptation. She had enough responsibility and more than enough demands on her time, as it was.

Andrea paused in front of the house, wondering again why Susie had wanted her to stay her for a month, and why she had stated specifically—no work? Andrea had never considered herself a workaholic. She worked hard and had her goals and dreams, but she knew how to relax. She had an active social life. Why, she wondered, sinking down onto the steps to watch the sunset, would Susie want her to risk indulging her worst fault like this?

For a moment Andrea thought about not answering the demanding ring of the phone. Phones were irritating contrivances, designed to disturb. And they did. But Mr. Andrews had insisted she have it turned on. "Ain't safe, missy, you being up here by yourself." Squinting through the shaft of sunlight dancing with motes she glared at the black box. Evidently there was only one way to stop the noise.

"Andrea? Andrea, are you awake?"

"Julie?" She squinted at the window. "What time is it?"

She had sat outside, watching the stars until late, and even then had been unable to sleep. She couldn't have been asleep more than a couple of hours, and those hours had been made uncomfortable by vivid dreams. She had tossed half the night, remembering her encounter with Bart Collins, remembering the touch of his fingers against her cheek just before he left. And the look in his eyes, which had said so plainly that he wanted exactly what she had wanted at that moment—to kiss her.

"Eight. Aren't you awake?"

"The time difference. It's only six out here."

"You're always up by six," Julie said.

"I'm on vacation," Andrea said. "I get to do strange things." Like imagining being held in the arms of a man she didn't even know. "So, why are you so excited and happy this morning?"

"Because I am." Julie laughed. "David asked last night and I said yes. I feel so . . . happy."

Andrea sat up slowly, a smile erasing the frown of a moment ago. Julie had been terribly disappointed last weekend, when David had only wanted to celebrate his latest business success, and Andrea had been furious that she was stuck in New Mexico, while her best friend was pretending not to be disappointed or upset.

"He did? Oh, Julie, that's really wonderful. So, tell me everything. Where did he take you? What did you wear? Everything."

"Well, maybe not everything." Julie laughed again, softly, then began a detailed account of the evening.

"It sounds wonderful," Andrea sighed. "I just wish I was there with you rather than stuck out here."

"I'm not getting married tomorrow," Julie declared "You'll be home in plenty of time to be my maid of hono How does a Christmas wedding sound?"

"Beautiful. But Julie, please, no red dresses."

"Green, Andrea, to match your eyes. And you have to catch the bouquet."

"Julie," Andrea warned. But her friend just laughed again and said goodbye.

Pulling the blanket over her shoulders, Andrea lay in the cool, early morning for a long time. She did resent being clear across the country on the whim of someone who had once been her favorite person. She resented feeling angry with an aunt she had loved dearly. To obliterate the uneasy silence she finally got up and dropped a tape into the cassette player, fixed some coffee and curled back under the blanket, staring sightlessly at the empty fireplace.

When the cats finally demanded attention she crawled from bed, dressed and poured herself some coffee. She had another full day of sight-seeing planned, but she didn't feel like wandering through another store, shop, museum or gallery alone. For some unexplained reason she felt terribly lonely.

Feeling confined by the silence, she stepped out onto the sagging porch, shivering as the early-morning air brushed her arms and legs. Sitting down on the top step, she propped her elbows on her knees, rested her chin on the heels of her hands and stared pensively into the distance. It was almost cool enough now for a fire. Thinking of a fire made her think of Mr. Andrews and his less than subtle remarks about fires and shared meals, which only made her feel lonelier.

Bart walked, enjoying the majestic beauty of the Rocky Mountains and the stunning, fall colors that surrounded him. The aspens rustled in the soft breeze. He paused, inhaling the crisp air, then slowly looked down the valley.

It had become a habit, walking up to this ridge, to this spot. From here he could see the valley, Eagle Nest Lake, the tiny town of Angel Fire and the rock outcrop where he had last seen *her*.

She had not been there again, but he still found himself looking. His gaze moved in the pattern that had become bit, a pattern that suggested he was afraid to find her there, after all. He looked from his right, where the town lay, left across the sparkling lake and then up. She was there. Sitting on the rock.

Bart stood still, just watching, trying to deny the need to see her again. He honestly couldn't decide if it was simply because he found her so sexy and appealing, or if it was because of the flashes of understanding and compassion. The first he could handle. The second could be dangerous. Feelings of compassion and understanding could lead a man into the deadly trap of giving promises, only to find that all the supposed understanding had been a ploy to get attention. Slowly he moved through the trees, mountains and fall foliage forgotten.

Andrea became aware that she was no longer alone. The air had taken on the same thinness and clearness of Monday morning, though she had neither seen nor heard anyone.

"I was hoping you'd come back."

The quiet, deep voice came from just behind her. She could feel his eyes on her, almost like a touch. Her heart skipped a beat at the realization that what she had been hoping was that he would come back.

"Good afternoon, Mr. Collins." Only why had she wanted to see him? "I heard you've been asking about me in town." Had he really been watching for her, waiting for her?

"Reading your crystal ball again?"

She wished he would move, so that she could see him. She wanted to read the expression on his face and see his eyes again. She wanted to lose herself for a moment in those brown depths. She turned her head slightly, but he was still too far back for her to see him.

"I'm sure Zeke and Hal and Dave Benson are wondering about you. Surely you must realize that these people don't believe in witches and gypsies."

"How did you hear about that?"

"Just keeping up on current events."

"What else did your crystal ball say?"

"You forget, Mr. Collins, Friday is my day off."

"What do witches do on a Friday?"

She relaxed into the teasing banter. This was just what she had needed, a little lighthearted teasing. This was why she had hoped to see him again. For a few minutes she could forget her own doubts and questions.

"Friday is the day I do my errands."

He chuckled, the sound drifting into space. "I thought witches did their errands at night."

"Mostly yes," she agreed with a smile. "But these are the more human errands. The cats must be fed."

A full, rich laugh spilled over her and drifted off into the valley. It was like sitting under a warm, sun-sparkled waterfall of sound.

"How could I forget? All witches would have at least one cat. A familiar, I believe."

She suppressed her own laughter, pretending to be completely serious. "Of course." Her spirits, which had been at a low ebb all week and really at bottom today, began to lift with each moment.

"What do witches eat?" he asked.

"That, Mr. Collins, must remain a secret."

"On Fridays," he persisted, "on your day off, when you resume a more human form, as now, do you eat then?"

She turned completely at last and looked up from her rock. He was sitting just where he had been on Saturday, but there was a difference about him. He was more relaxed. His eyes were less restless. The tension in his shoulders was less evident, as well. Whatever stresses he had brought with him were beginning to fade. Andrea was surprised at how much that little bit of knowledge pleased her. If she had stopped to think, she would have been even more surprised that she noted all those things in her brief glance.

"If a believer in your craft were to ask you to have dinner, on a Friday of course, would you accept?"

She had been so lost in her own thoughts that she had forgotten the question until he asked again. He was asking her out. She couldn't go out with him. This much was fine, this teasing and bantering, but no, she would not let it go beyond this.

"No, that wouldn't be very wise."

Not wise, but so very tempting. She was lonely. She was bored. She was scared. And she was curious about this man whom she couldn't seem to ignore or forget. She would only be here a few weeks, and the attraction she felt was too strong to play with. It would be like playing with fire.

Bart didn't know if he was relieved or disappointed when she refused his invitation. She had more sense than he, obviously. He studied her from his vantage point. Today she was dressed in dark, somber colors, black slacks and a gray blouse. Her hair was gathered into a neat twist at her neck. The style made her look sad.

"Why are you sad today, Gypsy?"

Andrea turned at the question. The joking tone was gone and he was watching her with a gentle, questioning look. "Excuse me?"

"Why are you so sad today?"

Before she could muster an answer from the confusion of her thoughts, he spoke again.

"I think you're lonely."

# Three

——

I'm both sad and lonely, I guess."

"Why?"

"I don't want to be here," she admitted.

"Why?" he asked again.

"My best friend just became engaged, and I can't be there to share it with her. I'm bored to tears." Andrea responded unguardedly, surprised by his awareness of her feelings. "I'm tired of sight-seeing and coming back to two cats who could care less if I walked in a volcano or saw a beautiful painting. I just want to go home."

"Can't you go home?"

"No!" It was an unexpected experience to have someone sensitive to her feelings. His attentiveness and her loneliness combined to make her answers bluntly honest.

"Why?"

"My aunt left me that stupid house on the wrong side of the valley and said I have to stay here for a month before I do anything with it. But, the really stupid part of this whole thing is that she never stayed here herself. A whole month of time wasted! I've got things to do, people depending on me, yet I'm stuck here for a whole month.''

Andrea's face flamed as the last words tumbled from her tongue. She never had emotional outbursts. She certainly never had them in front of people she didn't know, and it wasn't in her nature to tell a person she didn't know everything she was thinking, as she just had. At least she hadn't mentioned the fact she wasn't sleeping because she kept wondering how it would be to kiss him.

Chagrined, her only thought was to leave before she said something worse than she already had. She was suffering from some strange form of cabin fever. She had already gone crazy without realizing it. Whatever was wrong with her, it obviously was not a good day to be talking to anyone other than the cats, no matter how boring they were.

In her haste to escape, she forgot about the loafers she was wearing. Her foot slipped on the rock. A huge hand wrapped itself around her wrist before she could even reach out to steady herself. That strange tingle raced up her arm and down her spine. She closed her eyes against the dizzying warmth and was lifted from the rock and into the circle of his arms, steadied against the solid wall of his chest.

''Be careful, Gypsy,'' Bart said, using the excuse to hold her in his arms. He had tried to imagine more than once how it would feel to hold her slender body. Now he knew. She fitted perfectly. The top of her head came just beneath his chin. Her gentle, feminine curves stirred the blood in his veins, making his heart pound unexpectedly.

Andrea was mesmerized by the sensations. The heat of his body next to hers. The size of the man holding her. The strength of the arms that had lifted her with such ease, yet now held her so gently. His chest was broad and firm. She felt sheltered, protected in the circle of his arms.

It was a totally new experience for her. She had always been the one who sheltered others. Yet it wasn't an uncomfortable feeling. For the first time she understood some of what Julie had talked about when she had mentioned being cared for when she was with David.

Slowly she looked up, absorbing the sensations. Her head could easily rest on his shoulder; it was a delicious idea. She had never rested her head on a man's shoulder easily. The temptation was so great to experiment with the idea that she felt her spine beginning to relax. She felt small and helpless in his arms, a totally new sensation for someone her height. Carefully she held herself straight, refusing to give in to the almost overwhelming urge to relax against him.

She raised her eyes again, seeing the smooth, dark beard and then his mouth, his lips framed so temptingly. Maybe dealing with someone so tall wasn't necessarily so wonderful. His mouth looked miles away. *His mouth looked miles away?* She had definitely gone crazy.

"I'm sorry, Mr. Collins. I think I'd better go. I'm obviously not in the mood for company today."

"Don't go, Gypsy, please."

Her breath caught as his eyes captured hers in a soft touch. She couldn't have moved if she had had to. His eyes settled on her lips. Her breath caught again as his gaze lingered for what seemed an eternity. She wondered why he made no move to close the gap between them.

Bart was fighting the temptation to satisfy his curiosity. He could so easily bend his head, obliterating the few inches that separated their mouths. But her eyes held a flash of fear and her body shivered, whether from desire or not he wasn't sure.

"You're trembling, Gypsy." Bart touched her cheek, then gently tilted her face up. She avoided his gaze, lowering her lids until the long lashes veiled her eyes. "Please, don't be afraid of me. I would never hurt you, little witch."

Surprised, Andrea looked up. That was twice he had thought her afraid of him. She wasn't afraid of his size, but the impact he had on her senses was another matter altogether. This was an experience she wasn't sure she was ready to deal with. She wasn't even sure she knew what to do with the sensations that were racing along her skin and settling in the pit of her stomach as a dull ache. She did know that if she stayed in his arms longer, she would melt into a helpless mess.

"I'm not afraid of you, Mr. Collins." She stepped back a little, relieved when he didn't hold her, sorry that he let her go so easily. "I'm sorry I snapped at you."

"You don't have to apologize. It's refreshing to have someone say exactly what they feel."

Bart released her reluctantly as she stepped back and moved away from him. She was slender, her breasts small, high and firm, her waist narrow, so small he was sure he could span it with his hands. Her hips were small, but gently rounded. Some people might classify her figure as boyish, but she was definitely female. And he found her beautiful and very appealing. He ached to pull her back into his arms, to give in to the temptation and need to lower his mouth to the sweetness of hers.

Bart studied the woman before him. She was a changeling, elusive and difficult to define. Unlike most of the women he knew, this woman wasn't one-dimensional. One minute she was a laughing gypsy with bright red earrings and sparkling eyes. And then she was carefree and dreaming, sitting in the morning sun. Now she was full of anger, her clothes somber. Whichever guise she wore, he found her desirable. What was the witch doing to him?

Pushing the physical needs to the back of his mind, he moved back to the rock and sat down, pretending to look at the scenery. He wasn't sure what she was most upset about, having to be here, her friend's engagement or maybe something else entirely.

"Why did your aunt make such a request?"

"I have no idea." Andrea sighed. "It's not like her to do something like this."

"You said she was never here?"

"Well, Mr. Andrews, the man who looks after the house, said he had never met her. And I never knew of her coming out here." She thought about the rustic house with few amenities and couldn't picture Susie staying there even one night. Susie had liked comfort and ease.

Bart already knew that the same old man who was looking after Justin's house was also caretaker of the sweet gypsy's house. Bill Andrews had spoken to him quite bluntly about his questions in town. And Bill Andrews also had to be her "crystal ball," he thought with a silent chuckle. But why would the old man have told her about his inquiry.

Then again, Bill had given him a great deal of information about her. He now knew her name and age and the fact that she was single and only planning to be here a month. Was Bill Andrews trying to play Cupid with them? Not having an answer to that, he turned his attention back to Andrea.

"You miss your aunt."

Andrea nodded. She did. "Aunt Susie and I were very close. I'd do anything for her." Which explained why she had agreed to come. "I just wish I knew why she wanted me to do this." Susie knew how hard she had fought against the lazy side of her nature. Susie knew how hard she had struggled to overcome those natural tendencies to idle away hours in daydreams and fantasies. If imagining kissing a man wasn't fantasy, she didn't know what was.

"So you're stuck here and your friend is planning to get married."

"Silly, isn't it?"

"Which? Being stuck here or getting married?"

Andrea smiled for the first time. "Both."

Bart gave her one of those quizzical looks, his left brow raised. "You said you were unhappy because you weren't there to share it with her."

"Well, she's happy and that's what counts. Getting married the first time is a big event."

"The first time?"

Andrea shrugged and glanced around for some place to sit, her urge to run forgotten. "Face it, most marriages don't last. Everyone seems to do it at least twice." She moved to a flat rock not too far from Bart Collins. "Some do it only once and then spend the rest of their lives remembering their mistake with bitterness."

Bart was glad she was looking elsewhere. Her words surprised him. He hadn't expected the bitterness from someone so young and beautiful. "Have you ever been married, Gypsy?"

Andrea laughed at the question. "No. That foolish I haven't been. I have a lot of weird habits and a few wild ideas, Mr. Collins, but I haven't been that crazy."

"Most people consider being single 'living wild and crazy.'" Bart laughed.

"Most people are afraid of being alone. So they desperately search for another person to fill the silence, the hours, something."

"You sound very bitter for one so young," Bart said gently.

"I'm not bitter, I'm realistic. And I'm certainly old enough to know that there is no such thing as happily ever after."

Bart didn't believe in happily ever after, either, but he still didn't like to see her so disillusioned. He had a hundred questions about her past but didn't want to grill her, something he had been accused of doing in the past. "You are more afraid of commitment than solitude, aren't you?"

Angrily, Andrea straightened. It was okay, maybe, if he saw her sadness and guessed she was lonely. It wasn't all right for him to see her inner self that clearly. She really did have cabin fever if she was talking this openly with a stranger. She cast a lingering look into the valley. The sun had slipped behind the mountains and the shadows stretched in a deep, purple pool, ever deepening as they climbed the hill. She had just managed to waste another entire day, and it was past time for her to have left.

"I'd better go now."

"Are you afraid of my company, Gypsy?"

"It will be dark soon." He gave her another of those raised-brow looks, this time questioning and disbelieving at the same moment. "And I don't like it when people can see through me so easily," she admitted.

She stood, walking away, but not far. She wasn't sure if it was her or if he could just read people that well. No, it had to be her. Good heavens, she had practically shouted her anger about everything. How could he not help being able to see through her when she was handing him everything

Bart glanced at his watch. He didn't want her to leave yet. He enjoyed her company, her openness. He also didn't like seeing her upset. "It won't be dark for a while. Tell me about one of your wild ideas."

Andrea glanced at him and shrugged. She had already told him more than most people ever knew. He said he found her honesty refreshing, so she would share one of her most whimsical notions.

"I don't like clocks and watches. I hate schedules. I think people should just be free to do things as they want, not because a clock says it's time. Especially meals! Do you have any idea how awful it is to have to eat when you aren't hungry?"

"I've never had that problem," Bart admitted with a chuckle. "You could create total chaos without schedules."

"I know." Andrea sighed.

"So how far do you take this chaos?" he questioned.

Andrea looked up. "It was just a whimsical notion, not something a person should do."

"Why not try it?" Bart asked. "You could experiment, since you're going to be here awhile."

"I've already got twenty-four unscheduled hours a day. What I meant was under normal circumstances, when you have to stop work because you are expected somewhere. Or you're busy working on an idea and you have to stop because of an appointment. You have to make all you want to do fit into what everyone else needs and wants."

"So what you really want is to not have to worry about other people and pursue your own interests without interruptions?" Her life sounded pressured, something he could easily identify with.

"Yes, I guess it is," she admitted reluctantly. "As selfish as that is."

"It's okay to be selfish, Gypsy."

"How can you say that?"

"I don't think you should ever hurt another person, but don't think you should shape your own life to fit theirs, either. You have to be who you are. You have to be what you are inside."

"How do you know who and what you are inside?"

"You have to experiment sometimes."

"And what do you do if the experiment backfires?" she asked. It could so easily. She could become addicted to daydreaming and being idle. She could decide to run off whenever the fancy struck her, just as her father had done.

"Duck the explosion?" he suggested.

Their laughter eased the tension that had been building with his suggestions. She liked him when he was laughing. His eyes were so beautiful then, filled with glittering sparkles of gold and crinkling at the corners. And he had such a wonderful laugh. It was a deep well of sound that rumbled up and spilled so freely. So many men didn't laugh, as if laughter were an emotion like crying and they didn't know how.

As their laughter faded, Andrea ventured to ask her own question. "Do you have any wild ideas?"

"My ideas aren't that different from yours, except I do prefer a schedule."

"Don't tell me you set your alarm every night?"

"No, but I do get up at six every morning, and I like my meals on time." Bart laughed at the momentary disgust on her face. "When do you get up, Witch?"

"Whenever I want," Andrea declared.

"Liar," Bart teased.

Their eyes met and held for what seemed an eternity to Andrea, but she couldn't look away. Her heart beat too fast as the air stilled around them and his hand covered hers, warm and strong. His eyes moved over her face, staying far too long on her mouth. Andrea fought the urge to moisten her suddenly dry lips.

"Are you afraid of the dark, Gypsy?"

"No." She looked up at him. He was so tall. And so dominating. She had never really thought about the fact that her added inches gave her a degree of equality shorter women didn't have. And so warm. Even with the distance between them she could feel the warmth and strength that emanated from him like rays from the sun.

"The nights up here are beautiful. The mountain breathes and stretches up to touch the sky and stars." *Mountains breathing? He would think her insane now.*

"Would you sit with me then?" Not waiting for an answer, he took her hand and led her to a wide, flat rock. Together they sat, silently watching the world grow dark. The sky faded from pale blue to a deep iris and then slowly darkened to a deep, velvet blanket studded with diamonds.

Andrea wanted to watch him. She wanted to watch the strong features of his face fade into shadowy planes, to see the stars reflected in the brown depths of his eyes. She was aware of an utter stillness within him, a quiet that came from deep inside. Peace encircled them in a small cocoon, and the restlessness inside herself was replaced by contentment. She was where she should be, doing what was right. The world was a peaceful, unhurried place. Time was unimportant.

She shivered involuntarily as the air cooled rapidly, the setting sun taking the final, lingering warmth with it. His arm came around her, pulling her close to the heat of his body. How could something that looked so totally powerful be so gentle? Saturday she had thought it would be frightening in his arms. It wasn't. It was safe and warm and comfortable. Sitting tucked against his side was like curling into a favorite chair by a warm fire. She leaned into the warmth of his body, letting him support her, warm her, protect her.

"You're right," he said softly, his breath brushing her cheek. "The mountain does try to reach the stars. If I was taller I'd pick one for you."

"If you were any taller it would be impossible to—" She clamped her mouth shut just before the words "kiss you" popped out.

"To what, Gypsy?"

She was sitting alone at the top of a mountain with a man she didn't know, thinking about kissing him. It was definitely time to go home. "Good night, Mr. Collins." He didn't try to stop her as she rose and slipped into the shadowy trees.

Bart listened to the sounds of her steps, a twig snapping, the rustle of a branch. It had grown quite dark. Bill Andrews had warned him about the dangers of being out at night. It was his fault she was alone in the forest. He had talked her into staying past when she wanted to leave. She could easily fall or get lost.

He rose, calling to her.

Andrea stopped, her heart pounding. "Yes?" For the first time she felt a twinge of fear.

"I'll walk you home."

"I'll be fine." She could feel the tension, though she couldn't see his face. "Really, I've been up here at night before. I know the path and it's not far."

Bart reached out and touched her hair, wanting to insist. In the darkness his fingers found her face. "Be careful, Gypsy."

His thumb brushed softly across her lower lip before she stepped away. "You, too."

Bart listened to her move away, started to turn and then gave in to the urge to protect. It was a new response for him, one he couldn't explain to himself. He had never wanted to take care of another person before. Yet hadn't his concern for her feelings earlier been a different version of the same thing?

Not fully understanding his motives, he followed the noises ahead of him, listening for any sound that would indicate she was in trouble. All he heard was her steady steps. Bart came out behind her house and paused. He had no idea how to get back the way she had come. He also didn't want to frighten her by skulking around her house. Nor did he want to try to explain his actions. There had to be a road, he realized. All he had to do was circle around until he found it.

Bart found the road and began walking downhill. Gypsy was going through an emotional time. She missed her aun and obviously had very mixed emotions about being here at all. She had contradicted herself several times this aft noon. First wishing she could be with her friend and then saying she didn't believe in happily ever after.

Well, he didn't either. Five years of working as a divorce lawyer, handling some nasty cases, was enough to make anyone less than optimistic. What started as starry-eyed love ended in name-calling and greediness. He had reasons for feeling as he did and he wondered what had caused Gypsy to be so bitter. A love affair gone sour? No, it would be something deeper. She appeared too strong to have let one thing make such an impression.

And why was he wandering along a dark road at night, speculating about the life of a woman he hardly knew? He had no intention of becoming involved with anyone. She was right; marriage didn't last. Love was a momentary illusion, a chemical reaction between two people. And when the chemical reaction was spent, all that was left was bitterness. He wanted no part of it.

His body stirred restlessly at the thought. Sex for the sake of hormones was okay when a man was twenty. By the time he reached his age, he needed more in a relationship. Silently he admitted he did want the reaction, the sharing of passion. He just didn't want the bitterness and pain that always came later.

Andrea changed into a warm gown, turned off the lights and sat down on the sofa, a blanket over her legs. Mercury curled in her lap, purring softly as she stroked his fur. A small smile played across her face as she thought about Bart wanting to walk her home. That had been sweet, especially after her earlier outbursts.

Had she really said all those angry things? Yes, she had. She hadn't even realized she was angry with Susie until then, but when he continued to press for answers, everything just seemed to tumble out. Was it wrong to be angry with someone you loved and who was no longer there? She didn't want to be. But Susie hadn't been fair, asking her to do this.

Andrea knew she had a few bad habits, like her housekeeping—or lack of it. She could be neat as a pin in another person's home, but in her own she gave in to her tendency to sloppyness whenever the mood struck. She had some odd habits. Her erratic way of dressing was one. Of course, when she went to work, she dressed as well as any other career woman, choosing tailored suits and dresses that fitted the image she wanted to project.

But those bad habits and occasional quirks she could handle. She could tame them when necessary. But this, a month of idleness, wasn't fair. Andrea had worked hard to overcome her worst fault.

She was a dreamer. Just like her father. Unlike him, she hadn't let her fantasies overtake her. She had planned, made goals and made herself stick to them, even when other things looked more interesting, more fun or simply easier.

Susie had known how hard she had worked at overcoming that free-spirited side of herself. Susie had been there often enough to hear her complaints, to offer support or to listen to some of her wilder ideas to know it had not been easy to change. But she had changed. She had conquered the weakness she had inherited. She had learned to finish what she started and she was becoming successful in her business.

So why had Susie wanted her to do this? Why would Susie ask her to risk losing all she had worked so long to achieve? They were questions for which she didn't have answers. Questions no one but Susie could answer, and Susie was no longer here to answer them. It didn't make sense to her and she was angry. And hurt.

Sighing, Andrea picked up the cat and crossed the dark room, hoping she hadn't left anything lying in her path that would attack her toes. She reached the bed unscathed and slipped in, tucking the cat beside her.

At least Bart Collins hadn't seemed to mind her outburst. He hadn't even minded her ridiculous picture of a world without clocks. Andrea giggled as she snuggled into the covers. Imagine getting up at six every morning because you wanted to.

Andrea frowned, remembering his suggestion to exper ment. She knew who she was. Left to her own devices s would probably sleep till ten and stay up till two, and sp the time in between watching clouds drift across the sky. That might be who she really was, but it wasn't who she wanted to be.

The noise came again, pulling her out of a deep sleep. Andrea struggled to a half-awake state, only alert enough to move her feet toward the door. She didn't think to check to see who might be on the other side; no one had come to the house other than Mr. Andrews. Mr. Andrews! He was supposed to have come yesterday to look at the hot-water heater and bring some firewood.

Andrea opened the door and blinked twice. "Mr. Collins?"

"Gypsy?"

Andrea pushed her hair back, trying to wake up. "What... I mean why...? Uh—" Bart's deep chuckle interrupted whatever thoughts she might have been able to form, leaving her tingling down to the tips of her bare toes.

"I didn't mean to wake you," he said, still chuckling. "I came to ask if you would like to go on a picnic."

"A picnic?"

"Maybe I should suggest a late breakfast instead." His eyes swept the length of her. "Are you always this alert when you wake up?"

Andrea shook her head. Usually her mind functioned much better. And usually her body was numb. This morning things were reversed, her mind being a total blank and her body awake and alive beneath his gaze. The long gown she had put on last night felt as thin as tissue paper. Her skin still tingled as if his fingers had touched her.

"Would you mind waiting out here a few minutes?" There was no privacy in the house and she wanted to get dressed.

Bart nodded and she pushed the door shut, then hurried to the bedroom area of the house and tugged jeans and a sweater from the dresser, hurried back down the steps, through the kitchen, out the back and into the bathroom.

Bart tested the sagging railing on the porch before leaning one hip against it, admiring the magnificent view from the cabin. He heard scurrying steps through the house and then the opening and closing of the back door. Frowning, he turned back to the house. What in the world was she doing? He had just taken a step toward the door when it opened again.

"Uh . . . come on in."

"You dress fast, but why did you go out the back door?"

Andrea stepped back from the door. "The bathroom is out there, on the porch. Would you like some coffee?"

"Yes, thank you."

Bart stepped into the house and understood why she had asked him to wait outside. It was completely open all the way, from the unmade bed to the kitchen. His eyes lingered a moment too long on the tumbled covers, imaging her hair tumbled across the pillow, her body warm and soft with sleep. His own body tightened with the mental image he was creating of her lips slightly parted, her breath warm against his skin.

"The house is charming," he said.

Andrea looked over her shoulder. The house was in its usual untidy, dusty state. An old blanket lay half on the floor, half on the sofa. Books and magazines tumbled over the coffee table in a disorganized heap. The phone was on the floor. A dirty glass and cup were on the coffee table. Unwashed dishes were stacked in the sink. Good. Let him see she wasn't interested in domesticity.

Why would he even think she was interested in domesticity after her tirade yesterday? And after all that, why was he here at all? What was he doing filling her house, invading her space?

"May I sit down, Gypsy?" She shrugged and gestured toward the sofa.

Bart grinned as she tried to set a cup on the cluttered table. He took the cup from her. She sank into the rocking chair and pulled her bare feet up under her. "Do you have cream?"

"Oh, yes, I—"

"Stay there, Gypsy. I'll find it."

She shouldn't have found the laughter in his voice so nice. She should have resented the fact that he was finding her half-awake state humorous, but she didn't. She didn't even resent the fact that he was helping himself to the contents of her refrigerator.

Rather than finding his nearness intrusive, she found it pleasant. He filled the small house with his warmth and his scent. The house felt warm and comfortable with him in it. Andrea snuggled into the rocking chair, letting herself relax, not worrying that there was no conversation. Bart Collins seemed to accept her however she was. It was so nice not to have to be anything except who she was at the moment, and at this moment she was still closer to sleep than not.

Bart watched her eyes drift shut, the cup all but forgotten in her hand. "Come on, Gypsy. Drink your coffee. You're going to waste a beautiful day."

She lifted the cup to her lips and took a sip. "What time is it?" He grinned as she took another small sip.

"Almost eleven."

Her eyes flew open. "Eleven? In the morning?"

"Is something wrong?"

"Uh, no. I was just surprised." She had told him she got up whenever she wanted, but idling in bed was one of those things she never really allowed herself to do. It was hedonistic and self-indulgent. It was a terrible habit to get into, even on a vacation.

Andrea took a long drink of the coffee and started to get up to refill it, but Bart moved before she could, taking her cup, filling it and bringing it back to her.

"How did you find me?"

"I followed you."

"Followed me?"

"I followed you home last night."

Andrea straightened in the chair, not sure she liked being followed. "Why?"

"I was worried about you being alone in the woods at night."

Andrea studied him carefully as he spoke. Of course he was telling the truth. If there had been any other reason, he would have made his presence known last night. "I told you I would be okay."

"I didn't feel right, letting you walk home alone," he said. "What if you had fallen or gotten off the trail? You would have been out there all night."

Andrea shrugged. "I hope I would have had sense enough to sit down and wait until daylight, rather than go crashing around in the dark. And what about you? You were walking around in an area you were unfamiliar with. And I had no idea you were there. You could have been hurt, too."

That was one of the things he liked about her; she always thought of others, not just herself. "It's past. Neither of us got lost." Bart cleared enough space to set his cup down. "So what about it, Gypsy?"

"What?"

Again he chuckled. She loved the way his eyes crinkled with that soft rumble of sound. No, not loved, liked. She liked it. She would also like it if he disappeared as suddenly as he had come. She couldn't seem to think straight with him watching her.

"The picnic? I've fixed a fantastic lunch." His eyes skimmed over her slender figure. "I'm still trying to determine if witches eat mortal food."

Andrea knew she was playing with fire, or maybe nitroglycerin, but she was fascinated by him. She was no more able to say no to his invitation than water was able to run uphill.

"If you have plans I'll understand."

"Well..." She had planned to do some laundry and maybe even pick up around the house. And she needed to speak to Bill Andrews and apologize for not being at home yesterday. "Yes, I'd like to."

Bart smiled, flashing white teeth against the blue-black beard. "I'll get the Jeep and pick you up shortly."

"The Jeep? Where are we going?"

"A lovely place with a spectacular view. It's not far. I'll be right back."

Bart drove, watching Andrea from the corner of one eye. She still looked half-asleep, so he allowed her her silence as they passed through the town and out the other side, winding up and up until the road they had been following circled into a loop bordered by a high meadow. Bart parked the Jeep and climbed out, coming around to lift her down before she could finish undoing the seat belt and find the door handle. He took the hamper and handed her a large blanket to carry. She followed him across the grass to a point where they could look out over the valley.

The view was breathtaking. Below her was the town, tucked in its valley like a child's play set. In front of her and to her right the mountains marched onward to the north. Unlike her rock, this place was covered with lush grass. It invited. It was the kind of place one could settle into.

Bart set the hamper down and turned to take the blanket from her, spreading it in the warm sun. She wandered off toward the edge of the clearing, staring out at the vista. "It's a beautiful spot. How did you find it?"

"I like to explore. I thought you did, too."

"I do." Andrea turned, surprised to find him standing right behind her. "I just haven't made it over here before."

"It's called the Valley of the Ute. The Ute Indians used it for a summer camp."

She didn't think anything at the top of a mountain was really a valley, but the lush grass spread away between two peaks. "I don't blame them, it's just spectacular."

"Would you like to walk for a while or eat first?"

"Eat," she admitted.

Bart laughed, taking her hand and leading her back to where he had put the basket. "From the looks of your refrigerator, I don't think it's something you do often."

"I always get hungry at strange times," Andrea told him. "So I usually just fix something quick and simple. I don't like to cook."

"Or keep house," he teased.

"I'm not very domestic," she agreed.

"Then you really don't plan to marry and have children?"

Andrea wrinkled her nose. "I imagine I will one day. But I'm not in any hurry."

"No biological clocks ticking?"

"Nope." Andrea sat down on a corner of the blanket and pulled her knees to her chest. "Maybe it's selfish, but I really don't want the added responsibilities right now."

"It's not selfish to know what is right for oneself. We all come to reality in our own way," Bart said thoughtfully.

"Meaning?"

Bart smiled. "Meaning that what's right for one isn't necessarily right for another. One person may be content spending ten hours a day at the office, while another is content to live for the day, for the moment, and dare to try new experiences."

Andrea resisted the urge to tell him that the second description had nothing to do with reality. Nor did she tell him that the first description was a picture of her life, one that had made her happy, one that she would return to soon.

"Where are you from, Mr. Collins?" She accepted the plate loaded with ham, potato salad, pickles, deviled eggs and bread, trying not to gasp at the amount of food he had heaped on it.

"New York City."

"And what do you do?" His plate was now miraculously emptied of its contents. Where did he put it?

"I was an attorney."

"Was?"

"I quit. I was sick of it."

*I quit. I was sick of it.* The words seemed to reverberate through the sunny meadow, bringing a chill with them.

# Four

How many nights had she lain awake as a child, hearing those words or ones like them? How many nights had she tried to escape the low voices, her father's growing angry, her mother's tearful and frightened?

Mac had always seen a better opportunity, a more interesting prospect. The job he had at the moment was always a dead end or stifling and boring. The next one would be the answer to all their dreams. While he explained and planned, Tina cried. About rent, food, clothes, new shoes. Three children always needed something.

And Andrea had tried to be the peacemaker. No, not peacemaker. No one could talk to her mother at those times. So she had carefully watched how much she ate and never asked for anything. And she had listened to her father. She had been the one who supported, encouraged, believed and even understood.

She had understood her mother, too. They had never gone ~~h~~ngry, though their meals were plain, simple and some-~~tim~~es almost meager. They had never gone without clothes, though she remembered distinctly that last year, when she had had only five outfits for the whole year.

Then one night, when she was spending the night with Julie, her father left. All her mother ever said was that he had gone to chase his dreams. It had been hard after that. She was the oldest. She had to keep the house and her brother and sister while her mother worked. And she had worked, too. At first babysitting, and then in fast-food places.

She had taken her mother's advice to heart, keeping her grades high so she could get a scholarship and choose a career that was stable, rather than exciting. She had loved her father with the blind faith of a child, but she didn't want to be like him. She had never made a promise she hadn't kept.

And now, for the first time since she was thirteen, she was spending a month lounging, relaxing. And today she was spending it with a man who had quit his job because he was tired of it.

"What are you going to do now that you've quit being a lawyer?"

Bart shrugged and added more salad to his plate. "I don't know. Maybe nothing. I rather like your idea of a world without schedules and demands."

"The food is delicious. Did you cook it yourself?"

"Yes. I'm glad you like it."

"Maybe you should consider opening your own restaurant and feeding those of us who don't have talents like this."

He laughed, that warm, wonderful sound. "Too much work in that, Gypsy. I'm thoroughly enjoying being lazy and idle." Andrea ducked her head but he brushed her hair back, his fingers grazing her neck and sending a fresh tingle down her spine. "It bothers you that I'm content living this way, doesn't it?"

"It doesn't seem very practical or realistic," she admitted.

"You wouldn't be here at all if it weren't for your aunt, would you?"

"No."

"Why not?"

"I have responsibilities. A person shouldn't just walk out on people who are depending on them. And I have a business to run."

Bart wondered why she felt she had walked out on people by being here for a month. As he ate, he learned about the accounting firm that she owned jointly with her friend Julie. He could tell she was proud of what she had accomplished, but also worried about being away.

"Don't you feel comfortable leaving Julie in charge?"

"Of course I do. But Julie is planning for her wedding in December. I should be there, so she can take care of the details and not have to worry about the office."

Bart helped himself to another roll, wondering why Andrea felt she should be the one taking care of the office, while Julie took care of her personal life. Didn't she feel she had as much right to a life all her own?

"Who else is depending on you?"

"My family."

She had said she had never been married, but that didn't preclude having children. "Your family?"

"My mother, brother and sister."

With only a few more questions Bart learned that twenty-two-year-old Amanda and twenty-eight-year-old Rory had both graduated from college this past summer. Amanda had her degree in business, while Rory had a degree in veterinary medicine and had recently opened an office. Bart also learned that Andrea had helped them both with college expenses.

As she talked, he realized that she gave extensively of her time and energy. What he couldn't determine was if it was by choice, or if she felt obligated to them.

"Maybe your aunt wanted you to learn there's more to life than work and taking care of other people."

"I work hard, but I play, too. And I don't take care of ther people. They're my friends and family and I like being le to help them."

'Do you have time for yourself, Gypsy? Do you have for days like this?"

"I have a very balanced life. If I wanted days like this, I would make time for them."

"If you had taken the time to know yourself better, you might have discovered that spontaneity and an unstructured life are the keys to your happiness. Susie probably knew that."

"You didn't know Susie and you don't know me. You're jumping to conclusions," Andrea retorted angrily.

Silence filled the minutes as Bart ate and Andrea nibbled. She had been too defensive, but she didn't like the way Bart could see her very easily while she saw so little. She needed to know more about him.

"Did you specialize in a particular area of law?"

"Divorce."

It would help if he gave her more than one-word answers. "Have you ever been married?"

"No."

The response was so curt and cold that Andrea nearly dropped her glass. She glanced across the space that separated them, but he had withdrawn into himself, his eyes dark and brooding.

She was reminded of last Saturday, when the pain had been so evident. Maybe he hadn't been married, but he had been hurt. And handling nothing but divorces wouldn't have helped his outlook any. Andrea decided a change of subject was in order, but she was too curious about what had caused his reaction to think of one. Instead, she ate in silence.

She studied him while she ate, wondering if he had had the beard when he practiced law, of if it was a statement of protest, a way of separating himself from what he had been. His hair was a little too long for a lawyer, too.

"Have you had the beard a long time?"

Bart chuckled, his eyes filling with teasing laughter. Andrea flushed. The silence had stretched too long, but she had meant to say something light, not personal.

"Do you like it, Gypsy?"

"It's . . . it's very nice."

Bart reached out and lightly touched her cheek. "Are you curious, little witch?"

His fingers practically burned her already overheated skin. "Curious? About how it would feel?"

"No!" She lied.

"I'm curious." Lightly he touched her lower lip, tracing it from corner to corner. "I'm curious about how your mouth would taste. About how you would feel in my arms."

She already knew how it would feel to be in his arms. He had held her yesterday and it had been perfect. His arms were strong, his chest broad and his shoulders the perfect height. She knew because she had imagined it, even dreamed it. It would be warm, intoxicating and dangerous.

His fingers slipped into her hair, twining through the waves. "I'm curious about how your hair would feel spilling across my chest." His hand left her hair, caressing her cheek, then cupping her face in strong but gentle fingers. "But mostly I'm curious about this."

His mouth moved to her cheek, the touches butterfly soft. She was enthralled by him, entranced by the deep voice, by the warmth of his breath against her skin, the fantasy touches of his lips. She lifted her face slightly, seeking his lips. Her hands moved to his head, guiding him to her mouth.

He teased her with small kisses, and tantalizing caresses that made her thirst for more. She closed her eyes a moment to clear her mind, but it was too late—she had already leaned into his embrace. For a moment she held herself very still, then he pulled her closer. She was lost in a world that sparkled and danced like water over rocks, yet blazed and scorched like desert sand at midday.

His lips brushed her forehead, the beard first rough, then smooth against her skin. Her eyes closed again and she forgot to breathe. Small, feathery kisses fell across her cheek, coming ever nearer to her lips, which parted slightly with expectation. She moved against him, a soft whimper slip-ing mindlessly from her throat, lips parting in invitation. The invitation was accepted instantly as he claimed her mouth, his tongue slipping inside to seek with caressing tenderness each point that would give her pleasure.

Her breath came back in a rush, filled with a scent as fresh as pine, yet warm and musky as the forest floor. The heat that radiated from his body was as hot as any summer sun. And the lips against hers were draining everything from her until she clung, reeling in a world she had never visited before. Her hands moved as if with a will of their own, upward across the hard lines of muscles beneath his shirt, up to his shoulders to cling desperately against the breathless dizziness that was overwhelming her.

Slowly he withdrew his lips from hers, but his hands continued a deliberate, sensual exploration of her upper spine.

She reached up and let two fingers touch his mouth; the palm of her hand caressed the beard. Suddenly she came back to earth. This was total insanity. She didn't care what he thought. She only knew she had to get away. Panic pounded through her veins. He didn't try to hold her physically. His hands dropped away with the first flex of her muscles.

"Gypsy?"

His voice was rough and deep, a hoarse whisper that sent a tremor racing through her body to settle in some focal point deep inside her. What was this man doing to her? Andrea sat up and straightened her shirt, fighting for control of muscles too weak to let her stand.

"I'd like to go back now."

"Why, Gypsy?"

"This—" she gestured about the meadow "—is just an interlude. You'll be going back and I'll be returning home."

"That doesn't mean we can't enjoy the moment."

Andrea glared at him, then leaped to her feet and strode across the grass to gaze out over the mountains. Perhaps she had given him the wrong impression. Slowly she turned and faced him.

"Mr. Collins. I am not looking for a commitment, but I'm also not going to 'enjoy the moment.' I take myself more seriously than that."

"And I worded that very badly," he said, crossing to her. "I didn't mean it the way it sounded."

"Didn't you?"

Did he? He wasn't sure. He was attracted to her, physically drawn to her in a way he had never been before. He didn't believe in commitments. He didn't even know what he was going to do with the next thirty-five years of his life.

"I'll take you back."

Andrea watched him walk away, feeling strangely alone. She started to help him repack the basket, but he shook his head. She stood to one side, wondering what had made him withdraw into himself that way. Surely not just because she refused to have a fling?

She was thirty. She knew herself. Casual affairs, though she had only had a couple, had never been very satisfying, leaving her feeling empty. She studied Bart for a moment. Anything that happened between them would be more than casual, and that would mean she would end up being hurt. No, no matter how attractive she found him, she wasn't going to give in to the physical urges. It was too big a risk.

It was a silent trip back. No words were spoken. She wondered what he was thinking, but asking him, listening to the sound of his voice, gazing into the melting pools of his eyes, all would tempt her again.

In three weeks she would go back home, resume her job and the normal life she had always led. Bart Collins would probably be gone before then, if not back to New York, then to another city and another job.

The Jeep bounced over the last rut and came to a stop in front of her house. Andrea reached for the door, slipped out and turned to thank him, only to find him coming around the front of the vehicle. "Thank you for taking me." She didn't want him in the house. She didn't want to have to resist the fascination and temptation.

"I'd like to see you again, Gypsy. Maybe tomorrow we could drive down to Santa Fe."

"Santa Fe?" It was over a hundred miles to Santa Fe, which meant she would be alone with him all day. "I don't think so."

"I could pick you up early. We could have breakfast on the way and spend the day wandering through Old Town. There are some lovely churches there and several excellent museums."

"No."

"Why?"

"I don't want to." Andrea stepped back and walked around the Jeep, away from the house.

"Don't you?"

She knew he was right behind her, but she refused to turn and look at him. "No, I don't." No, she didn't want to spend a day in his company, resisting the temptation. "What is it you want from me?"

Bart chuckled softly. "I enjoy your company. I like your wild and crazy ideas." Gently he turned her to face him and held her, lightly but firmly. "I find you fascinating."

"I'm not fascinating. Sometimes I may just spout off whatever comes to mind for instance—wild ideas. It doesn't mean I live my life that way."

"Then I'd like to know how you do spend your life, what you want." He already knew how she spent her life—working and meeting schedules, demands and obligations. He wanted to teach her to relax, to enjoy this time that had been given to her. He tipped her face up as she tried to turn away.

"I want a chance to know you." Her eyes moved across his face, pausing on his lips. The green was tinged with gold-brown flecks, just as they had been when he kissed her. "And yes, I'd like to kiss you again." His fingers tangled in her hair as he gently tilted her head back.

She knew he was going to kiss her. She knew she should stop him, stop herself. His mouth came slowly down to hers. The contact was electric, overloading her resistance; her better judgment short-circuited and she gave in to the desire to feel his mouth on hers and his arms around her one more time. With a soft sigh her lips parted, and she lost herself in the magic he worked. She was pliant in his arms until she felt his hands under her shirt, skin against skin. She stiffened and tried to pull away, but his grip tightened, pulling her closer to him. She could feel the pounding of hi heart and the quickness of his breathing, hot and moist against her skin.

She pushed, pulling her mouth away and twisting her face aside. He trailed kisses across her face to her ear and down the sensitive skin of her neck, as if she had offered an invitation. Now her heart was pounding in equal parts of fear and physical reaction to him. At last she found her voice.

"Please stop. Don't."

He stopped the storm of kisses and lifted his head, his eyes smoldering. "What is it, Gypsy?"

"Please let me go. I don't want this." She was near tears but she wouldn't cry.

"Yes, you do." There had never been a woman who affected him quite like she did. Each time he had taken her in his arms he had felt stunned. She was captivating, interesting and refreshing in her honesty. He wanted to know her in every way. He wanted her friendship and her trust. He wanted her badly, and it was much more than the fact he hadn't slept with anyone for months. There was a reaction between them, a response that fed his desires. He wanted this woman. "And so do I."

She did want him, too much. Things were getting totally out of control. "Let go." She pushed against him once more. Her voice quavered and her eyes filled. "You are frightening me, Mr. Collins." She couldn't even consider what he was suggesting at the moment. She wasn't ready for what he was offering. She would never be ready.

"I would never hurt you, Gypsy, never." He ran one finger along her bottom lip. "You are the love you foretold."

"Me?"

He nodded. "Yes, you, my little witch." He kissed her forehead.

"Not me," she protested. "I'm too selfish. You wouldn't like me very much if you knew me." He would last about two days in her real life, before the schedules and demands became too confining. He wanted freedom, and she wanted her business and family and all the demands they held.

"I'm going to like you very much, my selfish beauty." Bart smiled as he smoothed her hair. "It will be, Gypsy."

Suddenly she was more than a little afraid. "Terror" was a better word for what she was feeling and "absolute panic" would be a close description. She was alone with a man she hardly knew. The phone Mr. Andrews had insisted she needed was inside the house, and Mr. Andrews was at least two miles away. "Nothing *will be*." She started to step back, but his hand tightened on her shoulder.

"Gypsy, how can you say that?" he asked as his lips touched hers with a gentleness that belied what was really happening.

Andrea panicked. It wasn't only the fact that he wouldn't leave, but also her own reactions that triggered the terror. "Don't," she said sharply as he pulled her close. Her hands balled into fists against his chest and rose to strike, only to be caught by his hands.

Bart looked down at the ashen face. "All you have to do is say no."

"I said no," she whispered. "Twice."

"Yes, you did, didn't you," he agreed.

"Then let go of me." He hadn't released his hold any. She was no freer now than a moment ago, and it wasn't just his mouth she had to worry about. There was the gentle touch of his hands, the heat of his body that enticed hers, the male scent that swept over her.

He had forgotten the shy, hesitant part of his witch. He had neglected the fragile side. "Look at me, Gypsy." He waited until she finally looked up. "You are a very beautiful and desirable woman, Gypsy. But I didn't mean to frighten you. I didn't mean to hurt you."

"You didn't—I mean, I—" There was no way to explain it to him.

"You don't have to explain." Bart stepped back, relieved to see she had regained at least enough composure not to fall or run off blindly. "I'll see you tomorrow, sweet witch."

Andrea refused to look back as she half ran to the porch and quickly let herself into the house, locking the door for the second time since she had come here. The first night in the house she had locked the door against an unknow mountain. Now she was locking the door, not to keep him out, but to keep herself in.

She leaned against the door until she heard the Jeep turn and the last sound of the engine faded into the stillness. Quiet enveloped her. Andrea took three shaky steps and dropped onto the sofa. The cats joined her, more than content to spend the evening curled in her lap.

Andrea tucked herself into the corner of the sofa and pulled the blanket around her. He wasn't the first man to be interested in her as a woman, but he was the first man she had been interested in in a very long time. His most innocent touch had the power to send her mind racing to far from innocent thoughts. Yet that wasn't what she wanted, was it? Did she want what would only be temporary, a week or two at the most?

If she was even considering such an idea, Andrea knew she no longer knew herself at all. She dropped her head onto the lumpy cushion and cried at last. She had never felt more confused or unsure of herself in all her thirty years.

Bart paced through the house, from kitchen to living room and back. Silent steps upon hardwood floors. The walls closed in, pressing down. Finally he walked out onto the back porch and stood staring at the sky. The stars had barely begun to shimmer, night hesitating one last moment before taking the earth for its own.

He had been crass and cold. He had treated her refusals as coy come-ons. Her pleas for him to stop had been just that. She hadn't been playing games, but neither had he. He was attracted to her. He did want her. That gave him no cause to treat her so roughly. Jamming his hands into the pockets of his jeans, he began walking. The silent tread that ate up the narrow road belied his inner turmoil.

"You're out pretty late."

Bart paused at the unexpected voice and glanced up, surprised to find himself in front of Bill Andrews's house. No lights were on, but he could distinguish the older man sitting on the front porch. He had no idea he had walked this far. he had only meant to walk to the end of the driveway and back.

"Good evening, sir."

"Come on up and sit," the older man said.

He wasn't in the mood for company. "Thank you, but it is late and—"

"She wouldn't go, would she?"

Bart paused. "No, she went."

After he had asked about Andrea in town, Bill Andrews had made it a point to speak to Bart, letting him know in no uncertain terms that he didn't think it appropriate for him to be asking idle questions and arousing people's curiosity. The older man wasn't going to allow anyone to hurt her. So Bart had told Bill earlier that he was going to take her on a picnic and feed her.

Bill Andrews chuckled into the dark. "You like your coffee black or with stuff in it?"

"Black is fine." He didn't want coffee and he didn't want to talk. Bart turned into the small front yard and mounted the wooden steps to the porch. He glanced at the chairs and then settled on the top step, staring at the dark valley.

"So she went, huh," Bill said as he set a mug of coffee next to Bart and returned to his rocker.

"Yes, sir."

"Then what's your problem, son?"

For a moment he thought the older man was being sarcastic, then he realized he was asking because he cared. Bart frowned, wondering if it was possible to care about someone that quickly, and then smiled. Hadn't he cared about Gypsy almost from the moment he had seen her? "I'm afraid I upset her." The older man laughed softly in the darkness, and Bart felt his anger welling up again. "I don't think it's very funny."

"Upsettin' her ain't the same as hurtin' her, son."

The rocker creaked into motion again. Bart sipped the coffee, wincing as the strong, bitter brew scalded his tongue. Bill Andrews made a mean pot of coffee. The creak stopped abruptly.

"Long as it's only gettin' upset."

Bart related what had happened, recognizing Bill's underlying need to protect Andrea, however, he didn't enjoy admitting to that side of his nature. He had always prided himself on being a gentleman.

"Got it bad, don't you, son."

Bart nodded, not willing to admit to the older man how attracted he was to the little witch.

"So, what you goin' to do about it?"

"I don't know," he confessed.

"She's just here for a spell. Says it's just 'cause her aunt wrote it down this way. Ain't planning to stay, ya know. Got her family and all back home."

Bart glanced over his shoulder. He knew what the older man was telling him, that it wouldn't be more than a temporary fling. "Maybe I want more than that," he said after a moment. Did he? He didn't want to make or be given promises that would be broken.

"'Maybe' ain't good enough,' Bill said firmly.

"She doesn't want more than that," Bart snapped. "She doesn't think love and marriage is any more reasonable than I do."

"If she didn't want more than that, why ain't you up there, where you want to be? And if you didn't want more, why ain't you out finding yourself a willing woman?"

Bart didn't have an answer for those questions. He sipped the bitter coffee in his cup, wishing he had asked for cream.

"How you goin' to support the two of you?"

Bart smiled, knowing that now he was being questioned as to his background. "I've got enough money to support us for a long time," he said into the darkness. "I was a lawyer. I'm not sure I want to practice again. I got burned-out on people fighting each other over the car and ripping children apart."

"Lotsa folks need lawyers for other things than divorces. Most don't have 'nough money to count, but don't mean they don't need some good advice. You any good?"

"I think so."

"Missy know you're a lawyer?"

"Yes, sir."

"How do your folks feel about you giving up a big-city lawyer job?"

Bart smiled into the night, thinking about his family. They had had their questions and doubts. But they tried to understand, and what mattered most to them was that he was happy. "They support my decisions."

"You're a lucky young man," Bill Andrews said quietly. "Your folks still married and happy?"

"Yes, sir."

"You're looking at things from one side," Bill said. "You've been seeing all the anger and forgotten that there is good out there."

"It seems to me only older people found that kind of happiness," Bart replied.

"We didn't have all the choices you have. Divorce weren't so easy back in my day. We had to make things work or be miserable. And there were a lot of people that was miserable. Ain't no commitment easy, son. Was it easy once you decided on all that schooling? Was it easy getting started? Ain't nothin' easy worth havin', including a good woman and a happy life."

Maybe he had been exposed to too much of the bitterness and disappointment people experienced when going through the divorce process. Possibly he had forgotten that love could last, like his parents and Bill's. It was something to think about. And tomorrow, when he was with her he would try out the idea and see how it felt. Finally Bart rose, realizing his anger had faded at some point. "Guess I'll start on back, sir. Thanks for listening."

Bill chuckled, and Bart heard the rocker creak rhythmically as he walked away, thinking about the old man's last words.

Andrea ignored the phone the first two times it rang, but the third time it started, she answered. She honestly didn't know if the feeling in the pit of her stomach was relief or disappointment that the voice at the other end was Julie's

"What's up?"

The house was cold and dreary. She stared without interest at the empty fireplace, wondering if Mr. Andrews had brought the wood he had promised, knowing she wouldn't bother with a fire, even if he had. She didn't feel like bothering with anything.

"It's that computer program we installed for the lawyers," Julie said. "I'm sorry to bother you, but I've spent the last two days trying to straighten it out and I can't. You know I'm not any good at troubleshooting these programs."

"Why didn't you call me sooner?" Andrea demanded.

"I tried," Julie snapped. "You haven't been home."

Home. She could go home, where she belonged. Her shoulders sagged with relief. She could get her feet on solid ground, at least for a few days.

"It's okay, Julie. I'll come home and take care of it."

Andrea spent the night pacing back and forth through the house, from the bed to the kitchen, kitchen to the front door and then to the bed again. The question that kept her sleepless wasn't the computer program malfunction that had caused one of her clients serious problems, but whether to return to New Mexico once the problem was solved.

At five-thirty in the morning she still hadn't made a decision. She called the airline and checked on flights. The cats twined around her legs as she wrote down times and flight numbers and cost. It would take her a day to pack and at least two twelve-hour days of hard, fast driving to get home.

She had agreed to stay here for a month. Susie had asked it and she would do it, if it killed her. If Bart Collins stayed the entire time, it just might. She booked a flight.

She packed a suitcase and took another cold shower, because the water heater was refusing to cooperate again. Dressed in a navy-blue suit, white blouse, hose, low-heeled pumps, with her hair pinned up neatly, and wearing the proper amount of daytime makeup she surveyed her reflection. She looked strange to herself, like someone dressed in costume. Recently, dressing like a gypsy had been more natural than wearing what had always been her standard wardrobe. She found her watch in the bottom of one of the dresser drawers and clasped its digital face to her wrist. A taste of reality was just what she needed.

It took one twelve-hour day to find the problem with the accounting program—the operator—not the program, as she had suspected. It took another day, thirteen hours, to straighten out the data and retrieve the figures, so the books balanced. Her eyes burned from staring at the video display terminal, and her shoulders throbbed from sitting over the keyboard. She spent a third day retraining the data-entry clerk on the program.

The evenings were spent with her family and her mother's sometimes subtle, but more often blunt demands that she stay home. The comments always included the veiled threat that she was going to be just like her father, if she didn't watch out.

The fourth day she said goodbye to her mother, promising to be home within a month. She spent six hours in the office, going over details and making sure things were running as smoothly as they could before she left them in Julie's hands once more. Julie drove her to the airport.

"I'm sorry to leave it all to you," Andrea said as she waited for her flight to be called. "It's not fair to you, especially now."

"The wedding isn't until December," Julie reminded her. "And I'm perfectly capable of running the office until then. Unless another computer screws up," she added.

"It wasn't the computer. It was that stupid girl they hired."

Julie placed a hand on her arm. "Andrea, what's wrong? You haven't been yourself at all since you've been home. Half the time your mind's been a million miles away, and the other half you've been grouchy and irritable and impatient."

"I'm sorry," Andrea said, glancing at her watch.

"You don't have to apologize, we're friends. Just tell me what's wrong."

"Nothing." Everything. All she could think about wa being back in New Mexico. She had found herself da dreaming about the house and the opportunity to sit

watch the clouds float across the sky. She had worried that
Bart Collins would leave before she got back. She had worried that he would still be there to be dealt with when she
returned.

"You've met someone! Haven't you?"

Andrea stared at Julie. "No. Where did you get an idea
like that?" Again she glanced at her watch, wishing she
could escape.

"From you." Julie laughed. "You're behaving just like I
did when I first met David. Daydreaming one minute, anxious the next." The announcement of Andrea's flight interrupted Julie. "Oh, darn! Andrea, you can't leave without
saying something."

"There isn't anyone," she said. "Really. I'll call you when
I get back."

As she buckled herself into her seat, she tried to convince
herself that she really hadn't lied to Julie. Bart Collins
wasn't a person she had a future with, even if she wanted
such a thing. So it hadn't been dishonest not to tell Julie
about her mixed thoughts. She spent the flight trying to sort
through her feelings.

She had known that going home would be a complicated
process. She had expected to meet with disapproval from her
mother. Tina had not wanted her to come to New Mexico in
the first place. She had really thought that the trip home
would clarify some of the mixed emotions she had been experiencing, but it hadn't.

As she drove through Taos and turned into Taos Canyon
toward the Mareno Valley, she admitted to herself that the
restlessness she had been experiencing wasn't from bore-
dom. She wasn't sure what was causing it, but four days of
hard work hadn't made any difference. She had felt just as
unsettled and irritable.

Andrea turned into Mr. Andrews's driveway, planning to
collect the cats. Instead she found a note addressed to her on
his door. She opened it and her heart couldn't seem to de-
ded whether to keep on beating or stop.

"Missy, went to visit my brother for a couple of days.
t has your cats. Take care, Bill."

"Bart has your cats." He was still here. And now she had to face him, whether she was ready or not. And she definitely was not ready. But if she waited, he might bring the cats to her, and she would rather meet him on her terms than his.

Not letting herself think further, she turned the car and drove down the narrow lane. The old Smith place wasn't old. It was a two-story modern house with cedar siding. She stopped the car and looked for a moment at the quiet structure. Swallowing back her sudden nervousness, she got out of the car and walked up the steps to the front porch. It was so very quiet. Maybe he wasn't home.

She smoothed her skirt and jacket into place, carefully ran a hand across her hair and tightened two hair pins before knocking, feeling more confident with each second that he didn't answer. She could get back into the car and go home, and get the cats from Mr. Andrews tomorrow or even the next day. Feeling confident Bart wasn't home, she knocked again. The door opened and there he was, towering over her, the key to her problem—only she no longer knew what the problem was.

# Five

———

Hello, Gypsy."

"Hello." Her throat was so dry that she could hardly speak. Her heart had tripped into overdrive and her stomach was filled with butterflies. On top of all that, she obviously hadn't adjusted to the altitude. The thin mountain air was making it hard to breathe.

"Would you like to come in?"

"No." She swallowed. "No, I just came to get the cats."

"Come on in while I round them up," he said, stepping back to allow her room.

"I don't want to interrupt you. I'll just wait here."

"You're not interrupting anything," Bart assured her. He leaned his shoulder against the door, letting his eyes move slowly from her neatly pinned hair over the tailored suit to her low-heeled pumps.

Her eyes had not left his face, but she couldn't read his expression. What did she expect to see there, great delight she had come to his house? What she saw was the warm, gentle humor she had begun to associate with him, an acceptance without censure.

"What are you supposed to be today?"

"I'm not supposed to be anything," Andrea snapped. "I'm just here to get the cats and then I'll go."

Before she could move he took her hand, only he took it with his left, pulling her minutely closer. She closed her eyes a moment as the now expected feelings raced through her and she was in his arms, her hand at his waist, his arms around her, holding her. For another moment she held herself very still and then he pulled her closer.

"I missed you, Gypsy. I thought you had left without saying goodbye."

It had mattered to him, she thought, surprised. Suddenly her hair tumbled free, the weight tipped her head back and his mouth was on hers.

Her world reeled as she acknowledged how much she had missed him the few days she had been gone. Her lips parted beneath the gentle pressure from his, hungry for the taste of him, for the heat of his body and the secure strength of his arms.

Slowly his lips released hers, but reluctant to let her out of his grasp, he tangled his hands in her hair. He watched almost hypnotically as he lightly sifted his fingers through the silky strands. "You should always let your hair be free, Gypsy. It's beautiful."

"The cats?"

Bart laughed softly, slowly putting her back. "I'll get the cats." He tipped her face up, his thumb brushing against her lower lips. "And I'm glad you missed me just a little, too. I just wish you would say it."

Bart brought the cats out and put the carriers and the food into her car. He held her door for her, not making any other move to touch her. Andrea paused and looked up Slowly, almost afraid to risk it, she reached out, letting h hand rest on the back of his for a moment.

"I did miss you, Mr. Collins."

Before he could respond, she slipped into the car an

Andrea twisted, tangling her foot in the blankets that she had already straightened twice. Jerking it free, she crawled from the twisted sheets. It was too much effort to fix the bed again when she knew she wasn't going to sleep.

She was too keyed up to sleep. Practically falling into Bart Collins's arms had totally shaken her. Admitting she had missed him had upset her. The brief trip away should have been the time to put things into perspective. She had practically fled Taos and Bart in a state of confusion, but the answers hadn't been waiting for her back home.

Andrea looked around the small house and groaned. She had left it in a mess, and it had managed to accumulate at least one new layer of dust while she was gone. She wasn't going to do anything but tangle the sheets if she went back to bed. Maybe what she really needed was some physical activity. She hadn't had any in days, spending all her time bent over desks, reprogramming computers. Yes, physical exercise was exactly what she needed.

The sky was turning a dull gray in the east before Andrea finished. Her muscles ached with fatigue, but the small cabin gleamed. Her head ached, and her mind was still in a turmoil. Andrea stood at the sparkling window and watched the dawn. It didn't promise to be any better a day than it had been a night.

Sighing, she turned toward the kitchen and fixed herself some hot chocolate and cinnamon toast. After eating, she carefully washed the plate and cup and put everything away neatly.

Andrea walked to the window again. It had turned cold while she was gone. And today was going to be wet. She watched the leaden clouds grow ominously dark, her forehead against the chill pane of glass.

It was the kind of rain that falls slowly, steadily, dully and drearily. No sudden spring shower filled with the joy of life. No angry summer thunderstorm to rage across the mountains. Just a steady, endless fall of water that turned the newly fallen leaves all the same shade of soggy brown and the rest of the world gray. Gray sky. Gray air. And gray nights. Even she felt gray and damp, chilly.

It was all his fault. Him and his talk of fortune-telling and her being something she wasn't. She had done the fortune-telling, but what had she talked about? Wealth and fame and love. That was what everyone wanted to hear. All that stuff about them needing each other and that he was going to like her was silly and stupid. But if it was silly and stupid, why had she tossed restlessly for hours and then cleaned house all night? Why, every time she closed her eyes, did she see his face?

"Simple, Andrea. You are a healthy female, and when a healthy female is kissed like you were, well..." So what was she supposed to do? Go throw herself into his bed?

*Something. I have to do something. I'm wasting time sitting here staring out the window.* She shivered in the chill air and got up to find a sweater. I could build a fire, she thought, but it seemed too much trouble. Everything was too much trouble today. Instead she dropped a cassette into the player and lay down on the sofa, pulling the blanket around her and waiting for the piano concerto to soothe her restlessness. Mercury curled up with her, warm and loving. She closed her eyes, one hand on the warm fur.

It was the cat that woke her, faithful watch-cat, with flattened ears and twenty claws pricking her to wakefulness just before the knock. Wrapping the blanket around her, she stumbled to the door.

"What do you want?" she snapped. Wasn't it enough that he had disturbed her sleep all night? Now he was standing on her porch, disturbing her music and her nap.

"May I come in?"

Did nothing penetrate with him? "No, I'm busy."

"Doing what?" He looked over her into the dusky, quiet room.

"Sleeping," she snapped. It was what she had been trying to do. She shivered as the wind shifted, blowing cold rain onto her face. "Go home, Mr. Collins."

"No," he answered cheerfully. As if she were nothing, he lifted her and stepped in, putting her back onto her feet before closing the door. "You sleep, sweet witch. I'll be here when you wake up."

Did he really think she could sleep with him in the house? "And just what do you plan to do while I sleep?"

"Take care of you."

Andrea stared at him, trying to understand what he meant. "I don't need someone to take care of me."

"Everyone needs someone to take care of them sometimes." Lightly he touched her face, tracing the circles beneath her eyes. "You're tired."

"Yes, I am," she admitted. "I didn't sleep well and I don't feel like company."

"I'm not company," he insisted.

"Then what are you? And if you think I'm going to fix you coffee or anything you're wrong. I'm going to sleep." She turned her back on him, dragged the blanket to the radio, turned the cassette over and lay down once again on the sofa, curling into the cushions. "Go home. I don't want or need you here."

"Go to sleep, Witch," he said and chuckled. "I'll be here when you wake up."

Andrea decided that the best defense was to ignore him. She closed her eyes, pretending he wasn't there, letting the music drift over her and shut out the cold day. Yet it wasn't the music shutting out the day. It wasn't the blanket making the room warm and comfortable, but she didn't want to think about that, either.

The music was still playing softly. A fire burned cheerfully in the fireplace, throwing light and warmth into the room. Andrea looked sleepily at the room and then, closing her eyes again, snuggled back into the blanket. But the momentary delight of a cheerful fire and soft music, counterpointed by dripping rain, was too quickly replaced by full wakefulness as she remembered. Him! She turned her head and found him sitting in the rocking chair, watching her.

"Hi, sleepyhead."

"Mmm." She had been rude and cold and very unfriendly, but there he was. "Why didn't you go?"

"Did you really want me to?"

'Yes."

Yes, she wanted him to go. He was dangerous. He was so very dangerous. She wanted him to go from her house, her mountain and the town. She would be content if he left the state. She had enough to deal with without this man. She didn't have time for him, whoever he was.

"Who are you?"

"Bart Collins."

She opened her eyes again. "No. Tell me about you."

He chuckled and settled back in the chair. "Bart Collins. Age thirty-six. Height six foot six. Weight two hundred fifty."

Andrea smiled in spite of the answer. "No, not vital statistics. Who is Bart Collins?"

No words broke the silence, but volumes were spoken in those endless sounds. His eyes held hers for a long moment. What Andrea saw there was as frightening as the words that followed.

"Maybe I'm the man who cares about you."

It was said so simply. "The man who cares about you." Could it really be so simple and so easy for him? "But you don't know me. You don't know me at all."

"That's part of the fun, Gypsy, learning about each other. I've thoroughly enjoyed this afternoon."

She knew she was staring at him but she couldn't help herself. He made less sense with each thing he said. "What did you do that you enjoyed?"

"I spent the afternoon with you."

"Probably the easiest way," she muttered, sitting up and pushing her hair back.

Bart chuckled softly. "No, it wasn't easy at all. What I rally wanted to do all afternoon was hold you in my arms and love you." He stood, turning to check the fire. "I fixed supper. Are you hungry?"

She felt trapped, caught in a maze, and each time she turned, she found another wall. Pushing the blanket aside, she got to her feet and again pushed her hair back. "I'm going to fix some coffee." Why was she telling him when it was her house?

"It's made. I'll get it."

"No!" He stopped. "What do you want from me? Why are you doing this?"

Bart watched her for a moment. He had promised himself last night he would not push. He would be patient and give her time and space. He hardly moved to reach her, one hand on her shoulder, the thumb lightly stroking the tense muscles while his other hand smoothed her hair into place. "I want nothing you don't wish to give. I did this because I wanted to do it. For you."

She laid her hånds on his arms. "Listen to me. Please listen. I don't want love or marriage or an affair." The desperation she felt was transmitted in her tight voice and the tense grip of her fingers.

Her life was too confused to allow time for Bart Collins. No. Her life was in a state of confusion because of Bart Collins and her aunt and this house. She was struggling to hold on to the person she knew herself to be, not to become something new. It wouldn't be fair to him or herself to let anything more happen between them.

Instead of letting her go, he pulled her into his arms and held her gently, strong arms protecting her from all the pain and coldness of the world.

"I'm simply trying to show you that I care about you as a person." She had looked so tired yesterday when she had come for the cats. Tired and very upset. "Nothing more." At least for today, he added silently. "Now, how about some of my famous potato soup?"

Andrea glanced at the kitchen. Curious, she walked to the stove and lifted the lid on a large pot. Freshly made soup simmered slowly. On a plate to one side were open-faced sandwiches.

"Where did this come from?"

"I made a quick trip to the grocery store," Bart said. "You didn't have any food in the house."

Andrea turned to the refrigerator and opened it. It was filled with food, as were the cabinets. "Dammit. You can just take all this junk with you when you leave. There was plenty of food in the house." He had even bought cat food. 'he would never be able to use all this before she left.

"Meat and fresh vegetables aren't junk food," Bart retorted. He pointed to one of the shelves. "Cold cereal and chocolate-covered peanuts are."

Andrea turned, hands on her hips. "I don't want to spend my life cooking. Bran cereal is nutritious. Read the label sometime. And everyone is allowed one passion. Mine happens to be chocolate-covered peanuts."

"Your one passion?" Bart teased, closing the short distance between them and cupping her face in his hands. "No, sweet Gypsy, you have more than one."

"Only one I'm going to indulge," she retorted.

"Then we should eat," Bart said, his eyes filled with teasing laughter.

Andrea ate, admitting only to herself that she was hungry. No argument she could think of seemed to make a dent in his determination. Only exactly what he was determined to do she didn't understand. Last week she would have sworn it was only to make a conquest of her, but even then she hadn't been positive. If possible, she was more confused now than she had been then.

The meal over, she stacked the dishes in the sink and went to stand in the living room. He showed no signs of being interested in leaving, and she doubted that anything she said would sway him. The wind gusted against the windows, leaving a coating of silver rain on the dark glass.

"Sit with me, Gypsy," he said, taking her hand and pulling her gently toward the sofa.

She didn't argue this time. There was no point in doing it. She sat down next to him and when he put his arm around her, she curled into the warmth of his body, leaning her head against his chest so she could hear the steady beat of his heart.

"You confuse me, Mr. Collins."

"Do I?" Lightly he stroked her back as she would one of the cats. "What have I done that confuses you?"

"Everything."

"Not everything, I hope."

The gentle stroking changed, becoming a sensuous caress. Andrea felt her body tremble in response. "No." Sh sat up, putting a little space between them. "Some things are perfectly clear."

"I think you misread a lot of things," Bart said, his relaxed position unchanged. "Why do I frighten you?"

"You don't," she denied.

"Just men?"

"Men don't frighten me."

She pushed herself from the sofa and went to the fire, poking it needlessly. Men didn't frighten her, not when she could put them into the categories she liked. Interesting dinner partners, good dancers, a good tennis partner. There were even men who were just plain friends. Bart Collins refused to be put into any category.

"I'm just not interested in any kind of relationship."

"Not even friendship?"

It would be absolutely rude to say she didn't want to be his friend, especially after he had fixed dinner, built a fire and more or less taken care of her all afternoon. It would be equally foolish to agree to anything more than they had. It was the kind of question that was incriminating, however you answered.

She turned from the fire, her face flushed from the heat. "I'll bet you were good in the courtroom."

The smile he gave her was absolutely wicked. "I'm very good." He laughed softly as her blush deepened. "In a courtroom."

Andrea replaced the poker in the rack with a sigh.

"Come sit down, Gypsy. You look worn-out." He waited until she had returned to the sofa, then gently settled her next to him, her head resting on his shoulder. "Was it a rough trip?"

Andrea related the details. He listened to her, really listened. And he picked up on the important issues, not the hours she had spent working, but whether the computer program was doing what it should and how difficult it was to use. She relaxed as she talked, letting the warmth of his body and the gentle caresses soothe away the tension in her muscles.

"The house looks great. When did you have time to do it?"

Andrea shrugged beneath his arm. "Last night. I guess I just needed the physical activity after being confined to a desk for four days."

Bart chuckled, his lips barely brushing her hair. "Yeah, me too. I chopped enough wood for two weeks yesterday."

They fell silent, the crackle of the fire and the steady patter of rain the only sounds. Bart inhaled the sweet scent of the woman in his arms, memorizing the feel of her against him. Her head was nestled against his shoulder, her body warm and soft against him. As she shifted slightly, Bart became acutely aware of her breast pressing against him and the length of her thigh pressed against him. Warm, sweet desire stirred in his loins.

Bart had pushed her once, something he still regretted. He knew she was only here temporarily. What happened between them would have to be her decision. He wanted her, but he wasn't ready to promise her anything.

"Gypsy, it's getting late. I'd better go."

"Oh." She straightened, pushing her hair back where it had fallen over one shoulder. "I'm sorry. I didn't mean to ignore you."

"I was enjoying just being with you," he said. "But you're very tempting, as is your house." Her eyes flew to the exposed bed as color stained her cheeks pink. Gently he tilted her face up, one strong finger under her chin. "And you need to get some sleep."

"I will," she whispered, aware of his lips just a breath away from hers.

His lips brushed hers with butterfly softness once before they settled firmly. She responded instinctively, wrapping her arms around his neck, her hands seeking the warm skin at his nape, then the powerful muscles that stretched beneath her fingers as he pulled her closer, leaning back so that she was resting against him. Again she thought of the forest, crisp and clean, yet musky with dark secrets. Secrets she wanted to explore. She relaxed into the cradle of his arms, her lips parting beneath the gentle assault on her senses.

Bart held back, sensing her hesitancy. She was a fragile creature who would need to be handled gently.

Andrea relaxed more, tasting and delighting in the textures and scents. The brush of his beard like rough silk against her skin, the moist heat of his mouth, parted against hers but not invading. She relaxed until his hand moved, slipping slowly up her side to cup her breast with gentle pressure. A river of fire flowed like molten lava from her breast to settle deep in her pelvis. She tensed, pulling away. He immediately freed her. She did not completely leave his arms.

Bart saw the hesitancy and questions in her eyes. They were questions he didn't fully understand and couldn't answer yet. Lightly he traced the shape of her mouth.

"You are an unexpected thing to have happened. Something very special and very fragile."

"I'm not either of those things," she said softly and straightened more, putting space between them.

"You are both." He rested his hand against the side of her neck, lightly stroking the line of her jaw with his thumb. He could feel the pulse jumping and the rapid lift of her chest as she breathed. "Do you know what I wish at this moment?"

She shook her head, not sure she wanted to hear the answer, yet she couldn't seem to completely break the web that bound them together.

"That this moment didn't have to end. That I could spend the rest of my life discovering all your wild and crazy ideas about life and living." He bent and his lips brushed hers ever so lightly.

He was telling her that he wouldn't be here long, that they didn't have a future. Time was a concept that she knew and understood. Her time was limited and didn't have space for this.

"Please go now, Mr. Collins." Go, before she could convince herself that there was time for him and a need for him. She had already merged him into her life too much, as it was.

Cupping her face in his hands, he kissed her again. "Good night, my gypsy."

"Good night, Mr. Collins."

He laughed softly, his hand lingering on her shoulder. "Gypsy, don't you think we should be on a first-name basis?"

She smiled and shook her head. She couldn't explain it, but he would always be Mr. Collins. It just was. It felt right when she said it.

"Then for you I'll be Mr. Collins," he said rising at last. "Sweet dreams, Gypsy."

She was hopeless and totally crazy, she told herself for the millionth time as she combed her hair once again and looked into the mirror. She had enough food in her refrigerator to last a month. She didn't need to go to his house for lunch. And if that was why she was going, what was all this looking into the mirror and brushing her hair? She didn't have to go. There was nothing forcing her to go.

But she was going. She had known this morning that she would. She had known last night when he invited her that she would go. She had battled with herself for hours, debating the reasons, but she was going.

It didn't matter that she found Bart Collins attractive. It didn't matter that she enjoyed every minute spent with him. But she wasn't having lunch with Bart Collins because he fascinated her, intrigued her. She had accepted his invitation to be friendly, because, like her, he didn't know anyone in the area. She was going so he wouldn't be lonesome. And she was going crazy if she believed any of those excuses.

She drove down the steep road and stopped in front of his house. After sitting for several minutes she reminded herself that she had chosen to come and she could choose to leave. With that thought she turned off the motor and set the hand brake. The sound of an ax falling with a solid thunk on wood was the first thing she heard. She paused, listening. It made her feel better to know he wasn't just sitting behind a window, waiting. He was carrying on wit whatever he would have been doing. She followed the sound around the side of the house.

The ax rose and fell in a smooth, rhythmic arc, broken only by pauses to put another log into place or toss the split pieces onto the stack. Though the afternoon was cool, he had removed his shirt, and a thin sheen of sweat covered his back and shoulders, highlighting each move.

His body was beautiful. No other word could describe it. Andrea stood transfixed, just watching. Muscles bunched and stretched, the skin rippling in response to the movements. There was not an ounce of extra weight, despite his claim to two hundred and fifty pounds. She had an almost irresistible urge to go to him and run her fingers along the outline of each muscle, to feel the skin slip over the bunching and stretching hardness. Instead she crossed her arms over her chest and moved into his line of vision.

He paused when he saw her, resting the ax against one booted foot. "I'll be finished in a minute."

That was fine. It gave her time to watch. She moved to the steps and sat down. Straight, black hair clung damply to his neck and forehead. His chest was just as magnificent as his back, though only lightly haired. His stomach was hard and flat. His jeans fitted snugly around his hips and thighs, the thigh muscles straight and hard beneath the fabric as he raised the ax, flexing and straining against the material as he bent his leg with the forward swing.

Bart dropped the ax and straightened, reaching for his shirt. He turned and caught her watching him. "What are you thinking, Gypsy?"

"Nothing."

"I think I like it when you think nothing. It turns your eyes somewhere between green and gold, rather like when we kiss."

Andrea hadn't been aware that her eyes turned any color when they kissed. She tightened her arms around herself and looked down at the ground, feeling her face grow warm. Watching him had been almost as pleasurable as a kiss.

"It's all right to have such thoughts. Don't be ashamed of them." He tilted her face up with one strong finger. "Never be ashamed of such things."

"I'm not." She wasn't ashamed of her thoughts, only at being caught with them so openly displayed. "I don't let myself do things I would be ashamed about." At least not yet, but nothing she had done with this man fitted into any realm of reference.

Andrea swallowed and looked away. "I shouldn't have come. This was a mistake." Things had degenerated too quickly to a level she wasn't ready to handle. She rose to leave, but Bart blocked her path.

"I am human, Gypsy, just as you are." His hands cupped her face gently. "I do want to make love with you and—" one thumb lightly touched her lips, stopping the automatic protest "—someday we will get around to it. Someday you will be mine."

Andrea stiffened, eyes blazing. "I will never be yours or anyone's, Bart Collins. I will not be going to bed with you and I most definitely will not be staying." She had known it was a mistake to come. She had only herself to blame for all of it.

"That won't change the future, Gypsy, it's a future you predicted."

"That as a silly game. A joke." Tears burned the back of her eyes. "I don't like to play games. I'm going back now and I would appreciate it very much if you would just forget we ever met."

Bart studied the vibrant hair that tumbled about her shoulders, the wide, green eyes now dark with confusion, the soft, full lips threatening to tremble. He didn't understand what was holding her back, but he had promised himself he wouldn't push her.

"Let's start over," he suggested. "Hi. I'm glad you came. Come on in the kitchen while I start lunch."

She followed him in without protesting.

"Sit down, Gypsy."

She slipped onto one of the benches and looked arou
It was a large, comfortable room with a trestle table set

the windows. An old pie safe had been converted to hold collectibles and was filled with different kitchen utensils, butter molds, hand beaters, teapots and other things. The work area was spacious and ultramodern, including a microwave and a self-cleaning oven.

"Can I help?"

"I'm only fixing sandwiches and coffee."

Andrea glanced about the well-appointed kitchen again. "You have a very nice house."

"It's not mine," he said, his back to her as he opened a large, well-stocked refrigerator. "I'm just borrowing it for a while."

Andrea sat quietly for a moment as Bart deftly sliced a tomato. The man certainly knew his way around the kitchen. "How long is a while?"

"I haven't decided yet."

Trying to find out anything about Bart Collins was as frustrating as trying to find hens' teeth. "Where are the dogs?"

"They belong to the owner of the house. Luckily, they're back with him."

"You don't like animals?" She had seen him pet the cats and scratch behind Thoth's ears.

"Not ones trained to attack."

Andrea fiddled with the salt and pepper shakers. He wasn't saying anything. Nothing at all, not even the owner's name. "I've asked before and you didn't answer me. I'd really like to know about you. What you plan to do, just general information."

"I did tell you. I have no plans at the moment. I'm just enjoying each day as it comes."

This was going past the point of reason. A person didn't continue to spend time and devote so much energy to another, who gave nothing in return. At least nothing of substance. He had given her his name, age and marital status. She needed something from him, something of him. She needed to know that she wasn't throwing herself away.

"You really expect me to just sit around with no questions until you decide to talk?" She shook her head in disbelief. "Mr. Andrews was right. I shouldn't be talking to strange men in the woods." *Or going to their houses for lunch.*

"Bill Andrews? Yes, he would say that." He chuckled. "I'm under orders to ask no more questions about you in town."

Andrea tried to picture the wiry older man ordering Bart Collins to do anything and couldn't. Bart Collins was too self-confident, too sure of himself to be ordered about. There was a sureness that said he knew what was right and wrong, the sureness of a man who knew who he was.

Only it was a false front. Men who knew themselves, who had concrete plans for the future, readily shared that information. Men who had a definite future gave you that information almost on meeting. Men who were stable and secure worked and kept schedules. She didn't know which to believe, the man he seemed to be or the man he said he was.

Bart put the platter of sandwiches onto the table and poured the coffee. "My idleness bothers you, doesn't it?"

Andrea accepted a sandwich. "Yes."

"Why?"

Andrea shrugged. "People should be responsible."

"Andrea, there is a difference between being idle and being irresponsible. It would be irresponsible if I were living on charity because I was lazy. It would be inexcusable if I were letting people dependent on me suffer." Something painful shadowed her eyes briefly. He was tempted to pursue it, but she turned away. "It's not wrong to take time out to learn who you are and what things are important to you and what I really want."

"Have you found the answers?"

Bart laughed. "I've only been here a couple of weeks, impatient one. Some men spend their entire lives searching for the answers."

"I know," Andrea muttered, thinking about her father.

"I was referring to our great philosophers," Bart said "Who were you thinking of?"

"No one in particular. But you have been here two weel Surely you've learned something in that time?"

"I've learned a lot. I've learned that money and power and success aren't as important as taking time to watch sunsets. I've learned I enjoy picnics in warm meadows. I think that is probably what your aunt hoped you would do while you were here."

Andrea bristled. Susie knew life wasn't about living in borrowed houses and watching clouds. Life *was* about schedules and goals and responsibility. "Don't presume to know things you don't."

"I don't want to argue with you," Bart said. "You're here because you feel you have to be. I'm here for my own reasons. I've lived my entire life making plans, pursuing goals and following schedules. Now it's time to find out what life is really about, who I really am and what I really want. Can't we just be friends and enjoy the time we have together?"

"Yes, I suppose so." It depended on what he meant by "friends" and how he wanted to "enjoy" himself.

"Good." He smiled across the table at her. "Then we can share the occasional meal—if you happen to be hungry—and maybe some sight-seeing, as well. Then you won't have to bore the cats with tales of your adventures."

Andrea smiled at his gentle teasing. "I have been giving mixed signals, haven't I?"

"One or two," he agreed, taking a third large sandwich from the platter. When he saw her look of astonishment he smiled. "Chopping wood is hard work. It gives a man an appetite."

Remembering the amount of food stored in her cabinets, Andrea knew he never had a problem with a lack of appetite. Any woman who took on this man had better be prepared to do a lot of cooking. And cooking and cleaning and taking care of another person were not things she wanted to do.

Before she realized what was happening, the afternoon was gone, having been spent in easy conversation and pleasant company. The sun was setting, leaving the house in cool shadows as Bart walked her to her car, his hand on her back. When he again suggested a day trip to Santa Fe she accepted, knowing she would enjoy it in his company. Then he proceeded to ruin the day with his next statement.

"You really don't know how beautiful and desirable you are, do you?"

"I'm not." He wouldn't talk her into anything with words, especially words as far from the truth as those.

"There will be time to teach you of beauty later." His kiss held no demand this time; it was simply a loving gesture. "You have a lot to learn, Witch."

# Six

And learn she did. Over the next week she learned to enjoy all the free time she had been given. She learned to relax and take each moment as it came. She learned to fill the hours without precise schedules.

But most importantly she learned about Bart Collins. She learned about the man, who was intelligent and knowledgeable. She learned about his easy humor. He was spontaneous, swinging her into his arms to dance around the kitchen to a song he said made him think of her, or suddenly detouring from their destination when something sparked his interest.

The overpowering man who had taken her on a picnic never showed himself again. But the sensual man who touched easily and often, the man who gave compliments with sincerity and held her close was there, teaching her of her own beauty and desirability. And one evening he taught her how dangerous it was to play with fire.

They had gone out to dinner and danced to soft music for ours. Andrea was relaxed, a little too relaxed. When Bart pulled her into his arms for what she thought would be a gentle, good-night kiss, the touch escalated. Her body melted into his, her mouth opening with a hunger new to her.

Suddenly aware of how close she was to forgetting everything but the heat of his body and the desire that washed over her so strongly, she pulled away.

"Don't tease me, Andrea."

His voice was low, almost threatening, a tone she had never heard before. Andrea stepped back. "I'm not."

"Aren't you?"

She hadn't meant to be a tease. Maybe she had had one glass of wine too many, or spent one dance too many in his arms. The passion had flared without warning and she had responded without thinking. "No!"

"I think you need to make up your mind," he whispered. "Your body tells me I can have you every time I touch you."

"Well, you can't!"

Suddenly she was spun around and caught hard against his chest. "Can't I?" One arm moved, but she was no freer than if he had kept both locked around her. His fingers traced her face, down her throat and back to her face before threading into her hair, tilting her face up to his. "I could and you know it." His mouth claimed hers with an elemental force that he had never used before. There was no holding back in his touch, no gentle, teasing persuasion. It was pure, hungry demand.

The world spun, then tilted like a top, then darkened as she was lost in a storm of pure desire, hers and his. No one had ever kissed her this way, kissed her with this hungry need, and certainly no one had ever awakened a reciprocal feeling of need within her. His lips left hers, tracing a path down her neck.

"Mr. Collins, I'm not ready for this," she whispered. Her own arms were locked around his neck. Her body pressed tightly to his, denying the words even as she uttered them.

Slowly he straightened, supporting her weight as well as his. Gently he lowered her arms and stepped away. His han came up to touch her cheek, then her hair. "Goodbye, Gypsy." He turned and left, closing the door very softly.

Andrea stood very still, not moving until long after Bart had left. Slowly the silence of the very quiet house settled like a weight on her shoulders. Shivering in the chill, she turned toward the bedroom area, slowly changed into a long gown and crawled into bed.

She had struggled all week to pretend that their relationship was no more than friendship, to pretend the kisses and touches were light and platonic. She had allowed him into her life, carefully pretending neutrality—and in one touch, one urgent kiss, he had shattered her pretense. And then he had left her alone to face the truth.

She wanted the experience that he had promised, both verbally and by his touch. She wanted to experience love the way he saw it. But she knew she was holding back for many reasons.

She would go back to Georgia, which meant a relationship with Bart Collins would be no more than an affair, and she wasn't ready to take that step. She wasn't sure she could turn her back when the time came. She could so easily fall completely under his spell. Whom was she kidding? She had already fallen under his spell.

But could she go home not knowing? Could she go back to the routines and the work without learning? She honestly didn't know.

She did understand that Bart Collins had said goodbye. She didn't think he had meant he was leaving the area. She had understood that brief message in his eyes. He needed her. He couldn't promise not to lose control. He wouldn't see her again.

She spent two lonely days at the house, mostly staring out the window, without finding the answers to the questions. And there were only two weeks left. She found it hard to believe that her views, her staunch position had changed so radically in such a short period of time. A week ago, would she have even considered continuing a relationship that would end? Would she have given two seconds' thought to deepening that relationship?

# FIRST-CLASS ROMANCE

*Mail This Heart TODAY!*

## And We'll Deliver:

**4 FREE BOOKS
A FREE GOLD-PLATED CHAIN
PLUS
A SURPRISE MYSTERY BONUS
TO YOUR DOOR!**

See Inside For More Details

# SILHOUETTE DELIVERS FIRST-CLASS ROMANCE— DIRECT TO YOUR DOOR

Mail the Heart sticker on the postpaid order card today and you'll receive:

— 4 new Silhouette Desire® novels—FREE
— a lovely gold-plated chain—FREE
— and a surprise mystery bonus—FREE

But that's not all. You'll also get:

## FREE HOME DELIVERY

When you subscribe to Silhouette Desire®, the excitement, romance and faraway adventures of these novels can be yours for previewing in the convenience of your own home. Every month we'll deliver 6 new books right to your door. If you decide to keep them, they'll be yours for only $2.24* each— that's 26¢ below the cover price—and there is no extra charge for postage and handling! There is no obligation to buy—you can cancel at any time simply by writing "cancel" on your statement or by returning a shipment of books to us at our cost.

## Free Monthly Newsletter

It's the indispensable insider's look at our most popular writers and their upcoming novels. Now you can have a behind-the-scenes look at the fascinating world of Silhouette! It's an added bonus you'll look forward to every month!

## Special Extras—FREE

Because our home subscribers are our most valued readers, we'll be sending you additional free gifts from time to time in your monthly book shipments, as a token of our appreciation.

**OPEN YOUR MAILBOX TO A WORLD OF LOVE AND ROMANCE EACH MONTH. JUST COMPLETE, DETACH AND MAIL YOUR FREE OFFER CARD TODAY!**

## FREE! gold-plated chain

You'll love your elegant 20k gold electroplated chain! The necklace is finely crafted with 160 double-soldered links and is electroplate finished in genuine 20k gold. And it's yours FREE as added thanks for giving our Reader Service a try!

# Silhouette ❤ Desire®

## FREE-OFFER CARD

**4 FREE BOOKS**

**FREE GOLD-PLATED CHAIN**

**FREE MYSTERY BONUS**

PLACE HEART STICKER HERE

**FREE-HOME DELIVERY**

**FREE FACT-FILLED NEWSLETTER**

**MORE SURPRISES THROUGHOUT THE YEAR—FREE**

✓ **YES!** Please send me four Silhouette Desire® novels, free, along with my free gold-plated chain and my free mystery gift as explained on the opposite page.

225 CIS JAZH
(U-SIL-D-08/90)

NAME _____

ADDRESS _____ APT. _____

CITY _____ STATE _____

ZIP CODE _____

Offer limited to one per household and not valid to current Silhouette Desire® subscribers. All orders subject to approval. Terms and prices subject to change without notice.

**SILHOUETTE "NO RISK" GUARANTEE**

There is no obligation to buy—the free books and gifts remain yours to keep. You receive books before they're available in stores. You may end your subscription anytime—just write "cancel" on your statement or return your shipment of books to us at our cost.

© 1990 HARLEQUIN ENTERPRISES LIMITED

PRINTED IN U.S.A.

**Remember!** To receive your free books, gold-plated chain and mystery gift, return the postpaid card below. But don't delay!

## DETACH AND MAIL CARD TODAY!

If offer card is missing, write to:
Silhouette Books, 901 Fuhrmann Blvd., P.O. Box 1867, Buffalo, NY 14269-1867

MAIL THE POSTPAID CARD TODAY!

BUSINESS REPLY CARD

FIRST CLASS MAIL    PERMIT NO. 717    BUFFALO, NY

POSTAGE WILL BE PAID BY ADDRESSEE

SILHOUETTE BOOKS
901 FUHRMANN BLVD
PO BOX 1867
BUFFALO NY 14240-9952

NO POSTAGE
NECESSARY
IF MAILED
IN THE
UNITED STATES

But Bart Collins had been right. She had a lot to learn. Now that she had the questions, she wished she knew where to find the answers. Mr. Collins could answer some, the most personal and intimate. But she was afraid to ask.

The weather changed once again, the crisp chill of fall suddenly becoming cold and wet. It rained. And rained some more, turning the narrow, winding road that led from her house into a slippery mire. Several times Andrea walked partway down the narrow track, wondering if she could get her car out, or back in, if she managed to get down the road.

And then the weather worsened, the wind blowing with an Arctic blast that her fireplace was incapable of warming. The rain was filled with sleet, spitting against the house. Andrea huddled before the fire, wondering if she should go down now, spend the night in a hotel or with Mr. Andrews. She was afraid to try to drive the slippery road.

The decision was made for her when the power went out. At first she thought she would stay. She still had heat, as much as she had had before. And she could manage to fix something over the fire. That decision held until she realized she had no water. Her water came from a well, and the pump did not work without power.

Dark gray clouds obscured the tops of the mountains as Andrea drove slowly down the winding road. She had never had her driving skills tested to the extent they were now. Between the slippery road, the glazing sleet and the gusting wind, she wasn't sure she would be able to make it. Her palms were damp against the wheel, her spine rigid.

The narrow track that led to the Smith place looked forlorn and unused. Her fingers tightened on the steering wheel. The house looked empty.

Andrea stood at the front door. Rain dripped steadily from the eaves, sleet pinged against her car and the wind howled forlornly. She knocked one last time before turning away, surprised to find tears burning her eyes. His goodbye had been just that. He hadn't stayed, not even two days.

Wrapping her arms tightly around herself, she went back to the car, pausing for one last look at the dark, empty house, oblivious to the rain that dampened her face or to the bits of ice that clung to her hair and stung her cheeks. She could go to Mr. Andrews or check into a motel in town. Then tomorrow she would... As headlights shafted through the rain, she began running.

Bart saw the headlights of the other car and began to brake before he realized it was Andrea's. His momentary joy that she had come to him this time was quickly replaced by panic as she began to run across the muddy distance that separated them. Bill Andrews was constantly worrying about her being alone and now, as he saw her pale face in the gray dusk, his own imagination leaped ahead along unpleasant lines. He swung from the Jeep and caught her in his arms.

"Gypsy? Sweetheart, what's wrong?"

The familiar vibration of his deep voice was sunshine. "I thought you had gone." She hadn't realized that was what she was thinking until the words spilled out. "I got so scared." She started crying, fatigue and relief combined.

It took every ounce of willpower he had not to laugh aloud with the joy he felt at her words. Gypsy might not be ready to admit how she felt, but she cared. She had turned to him and she had cared that he might have left. The rain felt more like sunshine to him as he swept her up and strode to the porch.

"It's okay, sweetheart. Everything will be all right. I'll take care of you."

She was incapable of independent action. He knelt and removed the wet and muddy boots from her feet. He pulled the damp sweater from her shoulders and set her on the sofa, tucking an afghan around her. She watched as he started a fire, then left, returning moments later with a large mug of steaming-hot chocolate. Only when she had drunk most of the chocolate and the fire was beginning to throw some heat into the room did he speak, his voice gentle and soothing.

"What happened, Gypsy?"

Andrea swallowed and shivered. "I lost power. The house was so cold with just the fireplace and then no power. It was so dark. And I didn't have water because the pump wasn't working." She shivered again and gratefully accepted the warmth he offered as he moved closer and once again took her into his arms. "And that road. That road was absolutely terrifying. I came here and the house was so empty. I thought . . . I mean, I don't even know when you're leaving and I thought . . ." She wasn't even sure which thing had upset her the most, her struggle with the elements or the thought he had left.

"I'm right here, sweetheart. I wouldn't leave you." His lips rested against her hair, his arm tightened reassuringly around her.

He would leave her. He would go. But at the moment all that mattered was that he was here, holding her. Andrea sighed and leaned against him.

"I'm going to fix you some supper."

"I'm not hungry."

"Have you eaten?"

"No."

"Just some soup then, to help you warm up. Then we'll get you in bed."

Andrea knew he meant only what he had said, but her mind leaped past the intent. She stood up, glancing around the sparsely furnished room. "I should have gone to Mr. Andrews or into town."

"There are three bedrooms, Andrea. You'll be safe here. At least for one night."

Andrea followed him to the kitchen while he heated a can of soup. He sat with her while she ate, and when she had finished, he led her upstairs to a small bedroom. After checking to be sure there were fresh towels in the bathroom and an extra blanket for the bed, he turned to her.

"Would you like something to sleep in or a robe?"

"No, thank you." Beneath her woolen skirt and sweater she wore a slip that would be fine for sleeping, and she didn't plan to leave the bedroom without being fully dressed.

"Then I'll see you in the morning."

Andrea saw his hesitation and knew he was waiting for her to make a move. "Good night," she whispered, slipping into the room and closing the door firmly.

Andrea lay in the strange bed, the blankets pulled to her chin and listened to the wind and rain. Why had she come here? she wondered. When she left her house, she had been thinking of Bill Andrews or a warm motel. Instead she had driven straight here.

She shivered as the wind gusted, blowing icy droplets against the window. Why had she run to a man she didn't know?

You do know him, a part of her said. She did. She knew she could trust him. She knew the important things, the things that made him special. He was kind, caring, gentle. He was fun to be with and reliable. She knew she loved him. Andrea sat up, shocked at her own admission. And then she knew why she had come to Bart Collins. Because she did love him.

Oblivious to the cold air that was chilling her back or to the wind pressing against the window, she sat in the dark room, thinking. If she did love him, then why had she held him away? Was it just because she was afraid of being hurt? Of having her trust broken?

They hadn't made any promises. None were expected. They both knew that if she took the next step, it would be only for now. He knew she was leaving. More importantly, she knew exactly what she was doing.

Andrea slipped from the bed, her toes curling in protest as they touched the hardwood floor. She pulled the quilt from the bed and wrapped it around herself.

The door squeaked as she pulled it open. Andrea stared into the dark hall. Slowly she crossed to the door opposite and raised her hand to knock, only to let it drop again.

She stood there, heart pounding, throat dry and toes freezing, listening for a sound, any sound. It was the cold that finally made her move. It was either go on or retreat. She knocked.

Andrea realized it hadn't bcen a knock, hardly a tap. The quilt slipped from her shoulder as she freed her arm and knocked more firmly, at least achieving a tap.

Bart folded his arms behind his head and stared up at the point where the ceiling would be. He knew he wouldn't sleep. Not tonight. Not with Andrea so close, so far away. Her sweet body was just across the hall, and no matter what he told himself, his body knew it. He didn't think standing in the freezing rain would cool his blood tonight.

Why hadn't he taken her to Bill, or driven her to a motel? Because she had looked so frightened. Because she had clung to him so sweetly and cried because she had thought he had left. What kind of fool was he to put himself through this agony over a few tears?

For just a moment he wasn't sure he had heard it. Then it came again, a soft tap, hesitant and shy. He flicked on the lamp, crossed the room in three long steps and opened the door.

The door opened and her eye collided with his bare chest. Slowly she looked up. She was thirty years old. She ran her own company. She dealt with people every day. But now she had no idea what to say or do.

He was glad he had put on the uncomfortable pajamas, though he doubted they hid his aroused state, which had only worsened when he saw her. The blanket she had wrapped around herself had slipped off one shoulder, revealing creamy-soft skin. One tiny strap hinted at mysteries yet to be revealed. Her hair tumbled about her shoulders, playing hide-and-seek in the edges of the quilt.

"Gypsy?"

"Did I wake you?"

"No." And now there was no chance he would ever manage to sleep.

Her tongue darted out, moistening her lips as her gaze slipped past him to the room beyond, before coming back to his face.

"I've got cold feet," she whispered.

Bart stared at her several seconds before he compre-
hended her words. "Do you?" His witch was shy, but she
had come to him. Slowly he reached out and drew her to
himself, his heart nearly bursting with emotion. "May I
warm them?" he asked, his lips barely touching hers.

"Please." Her toes curled again, this time from the power
of his kiss. Andrea lifted her hands to his shoulders, the
quilt forgotten. She didn't need the warmth of a blanket
when she had the heat of his body and the fire he ignited in
her.

She was hardly aware that her feet had left the cold, hard
floor until her back touched cool sheets. Bart came down
beside her, one hand resting on the curve of her hip.

"Ah, sweet, witch, how often I've dreamed of this."

She had, too, though she hadn't wanted to admit it. She
had dreamed so often of him looking at her this way, his
eyes soft with passion, hot with desire for her. How many
times had she dreamed of being next to him, warmed by the
heat of his body.

"Me, too."

Bart chuckled softly. "You could have fooled me."

"I was trying to fool myself," she admitted.

"You are a warm, passionate and beautiful woman."
Lightly he touched her cheek. "Let me show you that about
yourself. Let me show you how beautiful love is and you
are."

"Yes," Andrea whispered. "Please show me."

"My sweet gypsy. I need you."

There was more to the words than a statement of physical desire, but Andrea ignored it all, slipping her arms
around him and urging his mouth to hers.

Bart hesitated, holding back one last moment. "Gypsy, I
need to know. Have you ever made love before?" Her eyes
darkened and he gently traced the angle of her jaw, his finger coming to rest on her lower lip. "Please, I don't want to
hurt you."

"I'm not a virgin," she whispered, turning away.

"And what about the other?"

"Oh, I—" She hadn't even paused to think about it.

His lips met hers with the words; a gentle, questing touch as if he were memorizing their shape, their texture. He sculpted her face with his hands, exploring each contour. His lips followed, making their own paths along her brows, against her temple.

Words she previously thought she had understood took on a new meaning as his fingers played through her hair. He spent long moments tracing the shell of her ear and then moved to her throat, his lips warm against her skin. She was being cherished and adored.

Andrea tipped her head back as the heat in her veins built. It wasn't a flash of fire but a slow, steady warming. When he moved away from her she opened her eyes and started to reach for him. He hooked his thumbs in the pajama bottoms, his eyes never leaving her face. She would have moved to touch him, but his eyes held her to the bed and her arms felt heavy.

Andrea studied the broad shoulders, the muscular arms. His chest was solid and strong, the hair dark against his tanned skin. Every muscle was firm and defined. His stomach was hard and flat. She followed the thin arrow downward as he pushed the pants from his hips, bent to remove them and then stood.

Neither of them moved. He stood still, letting her gaze feast on him. He was magnificent. Slowly she came up onto her knees and reached out to touch him, her hands gliding over his shoulders. He caught her wrists, urging her from the bed.

He undressed her slowly, removing her slip as if he were uncovering a priceless treasure. He sat down on the bed, holding her hands as his eyes moved over her from shoulder to knees and back to her face. "You are even more beautiful than I envisioned."

Bart stood once more and opened his arms. Andrea stepped into the embrace and they touched for the first time—breast to chest, stomach to stomach, hip to hip, thigh to thigh. Their lips met as they sank as one to the bed.

Bart proceeded to adore her body, sculpting and molding with his hands and lips. Andrea lost herself in a slow, reverent exploration of him.

She was never sure when the intensity changed, shifting from a languorous heat to an intense hunger. Her blood hummed its heated way through her limbs. She gripped his shoulders, twisting beneath him, her body demanding. "Now," she begged. "Please, now."

"Yes, Gypsy, now." His voice was low and hoarse near her ear, his breath hot against her fevered skin.

Their bodies joined, but slowly. Andrea cried out in frustration, but Bart refused to let her hurry. He whispered soothing words and sweet promises as he held her. He guided, he set the rhythm, taking her slowly into a world she had thought existed only in dreams.

Andrea lay against the solid length of his body. She had never felt so whole and complete in her life. Unaware of the tears that were caressing its smooth, rounded contours, she pressed her cheek to Bart's shoulder.

Bart rose on one elbow and gently wiped away a lingering drop. "Do you always cry when you make love, sweetheart?"

"I don't know," she whispered, touching her own face in surprise. "I've never made love before, Mr. Collins."

"Neither had I," he whispered. "Neither had I, my passionate witch."

When she woke this time, the sun was shining in a brilliant, blue sky, but frost had settled into the corners of the windowpanes. She snuggled into the warmth and turned to study Bart Collins. It was a wonderful way to wake up, lying next to him, warm and snug in bed.

His hair had fallen forward over his forehead and she reached up to push it back, then lightly traced the contours of his face, the finely arched brows, the high cheekbones and straight nose. Her finger rested a moment against the full, firm lower lip and then she raised herself, kissing him lightly.

When he didn't move, she laid her head upon his shoulder, inhaling the masculine scent of his body. She had told him last night she had never made love. She hadn't, not like that. The first time had been awe-inspiring. The other times had varied; playful, curious, teasing, or simple passion, but always there had been that same, soul-shaking intensity.

Would it always be that way with him? she wondered as her fingers outlined each band of muscle across his chest, then drifted lower to the flat plane of his stomach. Slowly she slipped her hand lower to explore a muscled thigh. Even in sleep his muscles were iron-hard. On the return trip her hand brushed against him, his obvious arousal making her freeze.

"Don't stop now, Witch," Bart said.

"I didn't mean to disturb you."

"I don't find this disturbing." Bart chuckled, pulling her on top of him. "Now if you stop, that will be decidedly disturbing."

Andrea didn't stop. Bart let her lead this time, and though she didn't have the patience he did to prolong the episode, the result was the same, sublime experience.

Andrea dressed slowly, searching deep inside herself for answers, answers she knew she would need to face the morning and the next few minutes with Bart.

No, she had no regrets about last night. She found not even a twinge of discomfort. It was the thought of today and tomorrow that she found disquieting. What would Bart want or expect now? What did she want? That was what she couldn't answer.

The house felt chilly as she walked down the stairs, and she accepted the coffee he handed her gratefully. Slipping onto a bench at the table, she stared out at the frosty morning. A plate of bacon and eggs appeared before her. Andrea looked up with a smile.

"I'm really not hungry."

Bart sat down with his own plate. "You can't make major decisions on an empty stomach. You need something to fuel that brain of yours."

She shook her head, but picked up her fork and took a bite. "How do you know I was thinking about major things?"

"I could tell." He reached out and touched her face. "You get a tiny line between your eyes when you're thinking seriously." He ate a few bites. "Are you having second thoughts about last night?"

"No!" Andrea reached across the table, touching his hand. "No, I have no regrets." His fingers linked with hers. "I was thinking about having to go home."

"You don't have to, sweetheart."

"I have a business to take care of," she reminded him. "And friends and family expecting me."

"You can extend your vacation," he said. "Julie can handle things for a while."

Andrea shook her head. "I've left Julie all the responsibility too long already. She has a wedding to plan and her life to live. I can't ask her to do that right now."

"And what about your life? Don't you have the right to do what you wish?"

"I'm not ready to throw away everything I worked so hard to achieve." Andrea turned away and spotted her purse, where it had been left the night before. "I've got to go home and take care of the cats." She snatched the purse and slipped out the door before he could say more.

Andrea built a fire and sat down on the floor, waiting for it to warm the frigid room. The cats finished eating and curled against her to begin washing.

She glared at the two small animals. "I have to go back. It's not a matter of choice. Tax season starts soon, and I can't walk away then." Andrea picked up Mercury, cuddling him to her chest in trembling arms. "Oh, Merc. Did you hear what I said? Was I really thinking about walking away?"

She had obligations and responsibilities. She had made promises that had to be kept. She would be in Julie's wedding. Her family would never understand if she wasn't home for Christmas.

"What have I done?"

She knew what she had done. She had fallen in love with a man who didn't take responsibility seriously. So why had his flippant response hurt so much this morning? She had known what he was last night, before she took the step that complicated the situation further.

"Did I expect him to change because I did?" she asked the cat. The soft, rumbling purr was no answer.

Deciding she needed a shower, she gathered a warm gown and her velour robe from the pegs and dashed to the bathroom. The bathroom was unheated, and when the water heater wasn't working, as now, she doubted cleanliness was next to anything except pneumonia.

Despite a temperature in the twenties and lukewarm water, she bathed, then shampooed her hair, as if soap and water would wash away the doubts and questions and confusion. Finished, she snatched the gown and robe and a towel from the hook and ran back to the living room, intending to stand in front of the fire to dry and dress.

She came to a halt in the middle of the kitchen as Bart turned and looked at her. The clothes in her hand had not been picked up in a way that offered any shelter. "Don't you knock anymore?"

"I did. You didn't answer."

The floor was like an ice cube against her bare feet. "At least be enough of a gentleman to turn around."

"Is that all the heat you have?" he demanded with a dark scowl and a gesture toward the fireplace.

He'd been in the house often enough to know that. "Yes." He wasn't going to be a gentleman, and she wasn't going to die of frostbite, standing naked in her own kitchen. Lifting her head, she crossed to the warmth of the fire, laid the robe across the rocker and positioned the towel so it offered some cover.

"Andrea, for God's sake be reasonable. You can't stay here. You'll freeze to death or die of pneumonia."

"Don't try to tell me what to do, Bart," she snapped. She knew it. People always started telling you what you could or couldn't do as soon as they thought they had some claim.

He sounded just like a husband. Next he would expect her to be cooking and doing laundry.

She didn't want a husband telling her what to do or making demands on her time. She hadn't changed overnight. Her basic beliefs were still intact. She had responsibilities and obligations she would fulfill. She still didn't want a husband or commitments.

Laughing eyes held hers for a moment and then he kissed her, a kiss of pure joy and happiness. "I'll always know when you're angry, won't I? 'Bart' when you're mad, and 'Mr. Collins' when you love me." His rich laughter filled the room and he lightly brushed her cheek with the back of his hand. "Oh, woman, I love everything about you, especially the way that fascinating mind of yours works. I don't think I would ever be bored with you."

They would never know the truth of that statement, Andrea thought sadly. She didn't want more responsibility or promises, and without those they would never know.

"At the moment I don't care if you're bored or not. I'd very much like to get dressed." Her backside was going to be roasted while her front was freezing, and she felt very vulnerable, standing there with only the towel. "Just because I had sex with you, it doesn't give you the right to come in without permission or tell me what I can or can't do."

"We didn't have sex." Bart grated out the words. "We made love."

Even as angry as she was, she couldn't defame what they had shared. It had been beautiful beyond words. "Yes, we did."

"And that gives me the right to care."

"Oh, Bart." She reached for the robe.

Bart took the robe, draping it around her shoulders. "I'm pushing, Gypsy. I'm sorry." He took her into his arms, warming her front with his hard body. "I want to be with you, Gypsy."

"Bart, I'm the only female around here to be interested in, unless you have a penchant for older widows." Andrea reached up and gently touched his face.

"And you really think all this is just because I'm lonesome?"

She wanted to ease the situation, to leave things as they had been before breakfast. "I think it might be part of it. You and I have been together a lot in the last few weeks."

"I can promise you, Andrea, that is not why I want you. If it was, last night would have been enough." He slipped his hands inside the robe, stroking her back and hips. "And I do want you. Now. Again."

Andrea trembled, the heat of desire warming her. "We want different things from life."

"Do we? Don't we owe it to ourselves to know that truth, too?" He picked her up, turning toward the bed. "Don't we need to know that?"

And if they found out it wasn't loneliness, then what? Her future had been determined even before she came. "I'll still have to go back, Mr. Collins. My job is there. I have commitments and promises I have to keep. I'll have to go back."

"We'll work it out," he promised as he laid her on the bed and came down beside her.

Bart came back into the kitchen and stopped, anger building as he watched Andrea.

"What are you doing?"

She glanced over her shoulder. "The dishes."

Bart crossed the room and spun her around. He saw the fear flash in her eyes, but he was too angry to care. The plate she had been holding crashed to the floor, shattering. "Why?"

"They needed to be done."

"How many times in the last three days have I told you I didn't want you here to provide maid service?" he demanded.

"I wasn't—"

"Yes, you were. I leave the room long enough to take a phone call and you start cleaning up after me. You didn't eat tonight. You weren't even in the kitchen, so why in the hell were you acting like a slave again?"

"I wasn't acting like a slave," she said, twisting her wrist free of his grip. "I was simply trying to help." She moved across the room quickly and Bart knew she was putting distance between them. "I was taught to help and carry my share, not sit around like some harem girl."

Bart's anger cooled as quickly as it had surfaced. In the last three days he had learned a lot about Andrea. One fact stood out clearly. She took responsibility for everything around her. If he had let her, she would be cooking all his meals, doing his laundry and cleaning the house.

"I don't want a concubine," he said, moving toward her. "Nor do I want a slave, a maid or a housekeeper." Gently he took her hand, raising her wrist to his lips. "Don't you understand that?"

"Yes, but—"

Bart sat down on the bench, tugging her onto his lap. "No buts, Gypsy. I was taught that relationships were equal. It's as much my responsibility as yours." He glanced around the kitchen. Apart from the few dishes he had used making supper, it was spotless. "You never worried about your house having a few dirty dishes, or the bed being made three seconds after you were out of it each morning. Why are you so different here?"

"I was taught—"

"Forget what you were taught. We're adults. We're equals in this relationship." He cupped her face in his hands. "If I was married, do you think I would expect my wife to wait on me hand and foot?" He could tell from her expression that she did. "My God, Gypsy. We live in the twentieth century. Women have achieved some of their rights and more liberty than they've known in centuries."

"But women still have responsibilities," she said. "Ultimately it falls on them to be sure the meals are ready, the house is clean, the children cared for."

"Not in an equal relationship," Bart argued. "If I were married, I would treat it as a partnership. If you worked late, I would do the cooking, the laundry, clean the house. If I worked late, you would. And if we were both home, we would share the tasks, just as we would share the fun."

"I've never known any relationship like that," Andrea said. "That's idealistic, not realistic."

"Until you're ready to try a little idealism, stay out of the kitchen unless you want to eat," Bart retorted. "I'm tired of having this discussion."

"If I want something to eat, I'll just go home."

Bart chuckled. "Don't make threats you can't keep, Gypsy." He rose, keeping her in his arms. "Or I might just consider treating you like a concubine."

"Are you finished?"

Andrea didn't understand this man. She had never known anyone before who got angry because she was willing to do the work. His anger sometimes frightened her, but it always went as quickly as it came. Now passion flared in his eyes, hot desire that made her weak and glad she was in his arms.

"Just starting," Bart promised as he carried her up the stairs and put her onto the bed. "You wear too many clothes, Witch."

"If I didn't, you'd never let me out of this room, and I would be a harem girl."

"Yes, I would. I'd just have my wicked way with your beautiful body wherever you happened to be. In the kitchen. In front of the fire. In the shower." Her face flushed a soft pink. "Haven't you ever made love in those places?"

"No," she whispered.

"Then we'll have to correct that," he promised.

"Your house is too cold," Andrea protested half-heartedly.

Bart rose quickly and started to leave the room.

"Where are you going?" Andrea asked, feeling suddenly chilled.

"To turn the thermostat up."

Andrea opened her arms. "You already have, silly."

"Must need to turn it up higher," Bart teased. "You're still wearing too many clothes."

Bart watched as she slipped from the bed and stood, slowly unbuttoning her blouse. His heart beat with a heavy, slow rhythm as his blood grew warmer, humming through his veins with life. His breathing grew quicker as she reached for the snap on her jeans.

Her hair tumbled about her shoulders as she straightened. Her nipples puckered and hardened in the cool air. Bart felt everything inside him tighten with anticipation. "You're beautiful."

Andrea half smiled. "Too cold for you, Mr. Collins?"

Bart chuckled and began to strip off his clothes, tossing them aside, never taking his eyes off the woman who stood so proudly before him. He never knew who closed the distance between them.

# Seven

---

The days were passing fast now. She would hardly get up before it was evening. The time seemed to vanish with a blink. Each hour was beautiful and wonderful. Each minute was full. There just weren't enough of them.

Bart had said he wouldn't find her boring, but it was she who never found him to be that. He brought a fresh outlook to everything they did. She could sit and talk for hours; about books, movies, even politics. His law background gave him an advantage in the latter; her accounting gave her the advantage when the discussion turned to economics.

Every time she moved, he was there. If she decided to go for a walk, he was there. She was never really alone. He seemed to hear every move she made in the house. She would get up and walk into the living room and in seconds he would be there, his arm around her. He would build a fire. She would fix tea or coffee and they would sit talking, or sometimes just sit together, content without words.

And it wasn't that he hovered. It was that the minutes were so precious and so few. She didn't regret one second spent with him, one moment spent talking or sitting quietly. She regretted that there weren't going to be enough of them.

Head down against the cold, damp wind she walked. She had no choice. The time was gone. She climbed to the rock and stood for a long time, just staring at the winter-bare mountains, breathing in the cold air and memorizing the world around her. The leafless trees were quiet awaiting the coming season. The leaves that only a few weeks ago had been a riot of color and crackled sharply beneath her feet now lay in a brown, indefinable bed beneath a thin powdering of snow. The ski trails across the valley were wide and clear, waiting for the snow that would transform them into playgrounds.

She bit back the tears that wanted to form. She had known this day would come. She hadn't known how much it would hurt until now.

Slowly she walked down to her house. The rooms were damp and cold, yet it was warm with memories and dreams. The day he had fixed her supper and stayed while she slept, saying it was because he cared. The morning they had argued over where to stay. The morning he had awakened her to ask her to a picnic. And the other memories. Those of sitting and watching the clouds, the times she had thought of Susie and remembered all the wonderful times they had had together.

She packed all the clothes that were still there and carefully cleaned out the refrigerator. When she found a bag of chocolate-covered peanuts in the cabinet, she almost cried. Then she sat in the silent house for a long time.

At last she left and meandered down the path to Mr. Andrews's house. He always seemed to see her coming. Even now, with the house closed, he was out the door and on the porch before she was completely over the last fence.

"Missy, girl. What are you doing out on a day like this? Going to get caught in rain if you ain't careful."

"I wouldn't melt even if I did." She smiled. Some things in life would never change, and this old man was one. She was going to miss him, too.

"Now I imagine as how there's at least one around here might see it a little different." He grinned. "Come in and have some coffee."

She felt her face redden at his comment. Of course, with a man as curious as Bill Andrews, it wouldn't go unnoticed that she wasn't staying in her own home at night. "I'd love some coffee," she said, rubbing her hands together. "It's starting to really feel like winter."

"Feel more like winter when that rain starts," he said with a nod toward the lowering, gray clouds.

His kitchen was warm and homey. The old, trestle table was covered with red-checked oilcloth. Two rockers were drawn up near the window, and the air was scented with coffee and cooking. Andrea pulled off her jacket and hung it on a hook near the door. "I'll be going back in a few days, Mr. Andrews. I'll leave a check for the electricity when I drop the key off."

When he said nothing, she turned to stare out the curtained window. The silence in the room behind her was so heavy that she could hear the whir of the electric clock on the far wall. Suddenly the silence was broken by the splash of coffee being poured and cups being set on the table a little harder than necessary.

"Damned fool. Thought for sure by now he would have asked," he muttered.

"Excuse me?" Andrea turned to look at the older man.

"Guess we all make mistakes," he said, sitting down heavily. "I thought his intentions were honorable."

Suddenly she realized what he was talking about. She sat down next to him and laid her hand upon his. It was hard and callused, and his fingers were stained from the ever-present tobacco. "He's a very honorable man, Mr. Andrews."

"Hmph," the older man snorted in disbelief. "If he was honorable, he'd be after marrying you."

She shook her head and wrapped her hands around the brown stoneware mug in front of her. "I knew what I was doing. I wasn't tricked into anything."

She hadn't really known what she was doing. She hadn't really understood how deeply she would feel. But the fact changed nothing. It was an added pain to take with her, and she hoped it would be an added memory to cherish later.

"So you just play house together?"

Andrea flushed and looked at her coffee.

"I really thought that man could make you see some sense," he sighed. "I saw it the first time I mentioned him. A certain light in your eyes. Look at me, missy, and tell me you don't love him."

Andrea hung her head. She couldn't lie that much. "I love him very much."

"Then why are you leaving?" he demanded.

She didn't answer. He knew she had only come because her aunt had requested it. He knew she was going home, back to her job. She didn't have to explain it to him.

"You ain't figured out what love is at all, girl," Bill Andrews snapped. "You ain't even begun to understand."

"Mr. Andrews, Bart is the most wonderful man I've ever met." She turned the mug in her hand. "He knows I have to go back."

"When you meet someone so 'wonderful,' you make room in your life."

"My life isn't here. I have commitments at home, a job and family."

"And you don't have no commitments to this man you say you love?"

There was no point in arguing with the older man. How could she explain what she no longer understood herself? Andrea stood up and crossed the room to pick up her jacket. "We made no promises to each other."

Andrea paced from the kitchen to the living room and back, stopping to look out the window. She put the kettle onto the stove. It had been a mistake to move in here. Her instincts had been right. She shouldn't have done this; to him or to herself. The kettle whistled, swung her back to the present.

"What's bothering you, Gypsy?"

She jerked around, nearly dropping the kettle. "How long have you been standing there?"

"Long enough to know that something is bothering you. Something has had you upset for several days. Do you want to talk about it?"

"No."

His beautiful, brown eyes were shadowed with concern. The face she loved so dearly was getting the almost stern look he got when he was worried. She couldn't stand the pain she saw on his face, pain she was causing him.

She turned back and fixed the tea. For a long moment she stared out the window. It was spitting snow again. The sky was dull and leaden, the trees were bare. The world was bleak. Warm, strong hands settled on her shoulders.

"Talk to me, sweetheart."

She didn't want to talk. She shouldn't even have to talk. As she had told Bill, they had made no promises. So why did she feel compelled to explain?

"There isn't anything to talk about. I have to leave. It's time."

Bart sank into at the table, stunned. The words had hit him like a physical blow.

"When?"

"Tomorrow."

"Tomorrow? I don't understand. I thought you were happy here."

Tears filled her eyes. She hadn't expected him to protest her leaving. Their time had been a beautiful interlude, and both of them had known it was nothing more. "I can't stay here when I don't even have a job."

His eyes lightened for a moment, the golden flecks sparkling. He pulled her onto his lap. "Gypsy, I have money. More than enough to take care of you and those crazy cats."

She was trying to deal with reality, and he was still pretending the world was not made up of more than just what one wanted at the moment. "It's more than the money. It's my responsibilities and promises I've made."

Andrea took the few, difficult steps that brought her to him, afraid if she touched him, held him, she would never tear herself away. Lightly she touched his beard, letting her palm caress the shape. "And you will be making decisions, too. You have to decide what to do with your life."

He pushed her away. "That's what this is all about, isn't it? The fact I don't have a job, that I have no plans written in concrete."

"No," she denied. "It's not."

"Haven't you been happy?"

Her eyes filled with tears, but she forced herself to answer him honestly. "I don't think I've ever been happier."

"But you'll go back anyhow? You'll leave what you love and go back?"

"I have to go back. You knew I would." Gently she smoothed back the one recalcitrant lock of hair that insisted on falling over his brow. "I'm not trying to hurt you, Mr. Collins," she said softly. "I don't want to hurt you, but you understand I can't stay."

He understood. He understood that each of her words was a lie. She said in one breath that she didn't want to hurt him, and in the next she was leaving. She touched him with gentleness, even love, and said he understood what he couldn't begin to fathom.

"Has all this been a game for you? Is it just a game you've been playing?"

She turned at the bitterness in his words. It wasn't a game. You could stop playing a game. You could pick up the pieces, put them into the box and go home. How did you stop loving a man? How did you walk away because your time was up?

"No, Mr. Collins." No game could hurt this badly. "I have to go. I don't want to hurt you, Mr. Collins." She let him pull her onto his leg again and leaned her head on his shoulder. "I never meant to hurt you."

"Stay with me, Gypsy. Don't go."

"Oh, Mr. Collins," she said softly. Didn't he know he was about to kill her by dragging this out? She wanted to scream and cry. She pulled away and left his arms, when what she wanted to do was run into his arms and stay there forever. "I told you I would have to go back, that I had obligations there."

"And you feel no obligation to me?" he asked softly.

Andrea turned to stare at him. "We made no promises. You didn't want them and neither did I. No, I have no obligation to you."

He knew he was hurting her. He knew he was being unfair, but the thought of her leaving was more than he could handle. She was special to him. For the first time in his life he wanted something more. For the first time he wanted a promise. He wanted a commitment to bind her to him. But the fear was still there, a lack of faith that prevented him from offering those same things to her.

"You've found what we've shared special. I've seen it in your eyes. I've heard it in your voice when you say my name. You love me, Gypsy. I need to hear the words."

"I can't, Mr. Collins," she whispered. How could she possibly say those words, then turn and walk away? "I can't tell you that."

He pushed her away almost roughly and stood up. All he had asked for was the words. It wasn't a commitment, but he needed to hear those words. If she had said the words, there would have been hope for them, hope for the future, but she wouldn't even give him that.

"You were right. You are selfish. A selfish witch." He grabbed a coat from the rack and opened the door. "You want everything your own way, with no consideration of how someone else might feel." The door slammed behind him.

Andrea stood stunned for a moment, then ran to the door and snatched it open. "I told you I was selfish!" she yelled. "I told you you wouldn't like me!"

He turned, the ax in his hand. "Then go. Just go. Take your damned responsibilities, and go back to where they're appreciated. You don't even know an obligation when you see one." The bitter words were punctuated by splintering wood as he split the log with one blow.

* * *

Andrea turned and glanced at the clock, then regulated the control of the electric blanket higher. Time made no sense at all. A day was supposed to be the period of time it took the earth to rotate on its axis once. It was supposed to be a relatively stable measurement, divided into twenty-four hours, divided into sixty minutes, divided into sixty seconds. So why did each hour and day stretch endlessly before her? Two months ago the days had been gone in a blink. They had been like those scenes in old movies, where the pages of a calendar flipped quickly, gone before you saw them.

The earth rotated and the clocks moved with a relentless steadiness. What for others appeared to be a normal day, for her stretched limitlessly. It was a struggle to get through each endless, empty moment to the next and the next. If the days were hard, the nights were agony. Cold, empty, silent hours, with only her own thoughts and unanswered questions to keep her company. Glancing at the clock again, she turned her back to it and stared at the wall. Five o'clock in the morning was just too early to get up on a Saturday. She had a hundred miscellaneous errands to run later, but not at five in the morning.

Andrea turned and sank her teeth into the pillow. Nothing should hurt this much. Nothing. She no longer knew whether she had had a choice. Sometimes she wondered what would have happened, had she said yes and stayed. Sometimes she tried to envision what would have happened, where they would be, but it only made the agony worse. Those were the nights she almost cried.

Almost. But she didn't. She wouldn't allow herself that relief from the pain. She wouldn't allow herself to admit how much she had cared, how much she had loved and how much she was hurting.

Anyway, there hadn't been time for tears. The first few weeks had been so hectic that she wasn't sure she had felt anything. From the moment she had arrived it had been crazy. There had been Thanksgiving and then Julie's wedding, with the showers and parties, rehearsals and dinners.

And then Christmas and Amanda's engagement. There hadn't been time to think. But there had been time to hurt. It still hurt. Andrea threw the covers back. There was no point in lying here for hours.

Four hours later Andrea stared out the kitchen window at the drizzling rain. The apartment sparkled. There was not a speck of dust or one item out of place. She hated winter in Columbus. Why would anyone choose to live here? It was damp and cold. She hated damp and cold and wet.

She had never been bothered by the cold before. Maybe it was nothing more than being anemic. She would pick up some vitamins while she was out. She reached for her purse and the list of errands, just as the phone rang.

"Oh, Andrea. I'm glad I caught you before you left for the office."

"I wasn't going to work today. I have some errands I need to do."

"That's even better. I was going to ask if you would mind stopping by the printers and getting the proofs for the invitations. Oh, and could you pick up some milk for me?"

"I guess I can, Mom."

"If it's going to be such a burden, I'll do it," Tina MacLarson snapped.

He had been right about that, too. Andrea was selfish. She hadn't realized it until she came home, but she was. She had refused to do things, even simple things like adding a couple of extra stops to her errands. She had never felt her mother was a burden before, but now it seemed as though Tina was demanding, always needing her for something.

"I'm sorry, Mom. It's really not a burden." She wanted to explain. She wanted her mother to see her pain, to help her. But Tina would not understand. She would be angry that her daughter had so little sense. "I'm just a little tired this morning, and it's raining and cold."

"Maybe you should get a checkup. You haven't been yourself since Christmas." Andrea knew she hadn't been her old self since long before Christmas, but she didn't say anything. "With Amanda's wedding next month and tax season, you don't want to get run-down."

She didn't want to deal with tax season or her sister's wedding. She didn't know what she wanted. She just knew her life was empty and nothing was satisfying. It had been a hollow period, and no matter what she did or planned, it stayed hollow. Even her business, which had always been an escape, was no longer as rewarding as it had been before.

"I was going to pick up some vitamins while I was out."

"Good. Have you decided what to do with that shack Susie left you?"

Andrea felt the tears sting her eyes at the mention of the house. Her mother had seen the pictures and instantly deemed it a shack, not worth owning.

"Yes. I'm going to keep it. At least for now."

"Keep it?"

"Yes, Mom. I'm going to keep it." How could she part with a place that held such sweet memories? Someday she would want to go back. Someday she would want to sit at the rock and watch the sunset, watch the stars fill the sky like diamonds. Someday, when the pain had lessened, she would want to see it again.

"Andrea, that's the most foolish decision you've ever made. You could sell it and get enough for a down payment on a condominium or a new car. It's ridiculous to pay taxes and upkeep on a piece of property that won't benefit you in any way."

"I'm keeping the house," she said. "It's my decision and I've made it. It isn't open for discussion, nor am I interested in other people's opinions."

"Well, then maybe we can put it to use for vacations. Maybe Amanda would want to go there for her honeymoon."

No one was going to mar her memories. No one was going to share that place. It was hers. Susie had given it to her, and she was going to keep it. As it was. "No, Mom."

She hung up, while her mother was still sputtering over her refusal. She was just what Bart Collins had said; selfish, a selfish witch. He had also said it was all right to be selfish. She wasn't sure that was true. She wasn't happy being that way. She wasn't happy at all. Wearily she pushed open the door and headed into the cold, misting rain.

Andrea methodically went through the list of errands. Recently it had taken lists to get anything accomplished. Without them she found herself forgetting, drifting into daydreams, or just feeling it wasn't worth the effort. With the last chore taken care of, she realized that the last thing she wanted was to go home.

She didn't want to sit in the quiet, empty apartment. She didn't want to talk with an angry mother. She didn't want to participate in the plans for Amanda's wedding. She pulled into a shopping mall, parked and ran through the rain. Once inside, she wandered aimlessly among the crowds, not stopping to look or shop, just walking. Until she came to the travel agency.

The picture displayed so prominently brought a rush of memories, a wave of emotion so strong that she almost stumbled. It could have been taken from the rock or her front porch.

She had no idea how long she stood there, letting the memories wash over her. The crowds moved around her immobile figure as she recalled each day, each hour with him. At last she turned and crossed to a bench, sinking onto it, as tired as if she had just finished a marathon. Even her hands trembled.

It had been a silent catharsis, one that had raged internally, not accompanied by tears. At last she stood and began walking again. Realizing she hadn't eaten all day, she stopped at a snack bar for cookies and coffee. It was dark, but the rain had stopped as she left the mall. Andrea smiled sadly as the clouds parted and one small star shone through.

Each time he came back, he walked up here. First to the house. It was always empty, the small structure cold and forlorn, the wind sighing mournfully through the trees. And then to the rock, to stand and remember. And each time he was here, her words came back to him. "How do you know who you are? How do you know what you are inside?"

Without her he didn't know who he was. Without her he felt lost and alone. "When you live here, you may be or do whatever you wish. You do not have to talk about anything you don't want or do anything that makes you unhappy." When she had been here that had been true. Now nothing made him happy, and there was nothing he wanted to talk about.

Nine weeks. Nine long, empty weeks. So much had happened to him, so much she would never know. There were many things he wanted to talk to her about. He wanted to tell her about the time he had spent with his parents and sister over the holidays. He had felt the familial warmth and love in their homes, seen them through new eyes. For the first time in years he could believe in the promise of love. Their marriages weren't perfect, but they were lasting because there was a commitment to them and to each other.

He turned away from the rock and began walking again. Bill had the key to the house. Bart glowered at the thought of dealing with the old man again. For weeks he had been nagging him to call her, to go to Columbus, to chase her down. "She didn't love me," he muttered. He didn't know why he kept coming back or why he let the old man badger him, but each time he did just that.

Not only did he allow the older man to badger him, he set himself up for it, he thought an hour later, as Bill ladled vegetables into bowls and set a platter of fried ham on the table. But even a meal shared with a crotchety old man was preferable to a house that echoed with memories.

"You get all those contract things taken care of?" Bill asked as he set the last dish on the table and gestured for Bart to sit down.

"Most of them," Bart said. He had gone back to New York to sell his condominium and tie up the loose ends of a life he no longer wanted.

"Must help some, all that law trainin' you got."

"It helps," Bart agreed with a rueful smile.

"You goin' to be settlin' down here again?"

Bart glanced up curiously. This was the first time Bill Andrews hadn't said anything about Andrea. In fact, the entire conversation had been normal, too normal. He wondered for a moment what the old man had up his sleeve and then shrugged away the idea. Bill Andrews wasn't that kind of man. He came right out and said what he thought.

"At least for a while. I've been thinking about buying some land. Maybe that piece near the old fire road."

"It's a pretty piece, all right," Bill agreed after a few minutes. "But I prefer this side of the valley myself."

Bart chuckled. "You own this side of the valley." Bill Andrews might live in an old house and appear on the surface to be nothing more than a typical small farmer, but over the years he had used common sense and good judgment. The older man had a good deal of land and money.

"Yeah, and when I die, my boys'll just sell it off. They ain't wantin' to live here. I've been thinking about selling off a good part of it soon."

Bart slowly laid down his fork and then took a drink of coffee, trying to make sense of what the older man was saying. "You've got years of living left, Bill." Unless he was sick. "Why now?"

Bill shrugged and reached for a biscuit. "Prob'ly do. But I'm an old man. Ain't got the energy for life I used to. Just seems silly to me to keep on when I don't need to. I can put my feet up and stop all this workin' for nothin'. I just ain't meant for this here age we're living in, I guess."

"Why do you say that?" The older man was beginning to worry him. He had never heard Bill talk like this.

"Guess I just don't understand the world and people no more, that's all." Bill sighed. "Just don't make no sense to me. And I don't like to live where things ain't reasonable."

"Has something happened while I was gone?" Bill had spent the entire time he was fixing dinner talking about the local gossip, but he had said nothing that could account for this attitude.

"Nope," Bill said. "Ain't a thing happened around here, and maybe that's what got me so down."

"What was supposed to happen?" Bart had no sooner asked the question than he knew he had fallen into a skillfully laid trap. The old man didn't always just come right out and say what he thought. Sometimes he did play games, after all.

"What was supposed to have happened was you was supposed to bring that girl back here, where she belongs," Bill answered sharply. He got up and filled their cups, plunking the enamel coffee pot down heavily. Before Bart could reply he continued. "I ain't never, in all my years, seen two people be so stupid. First missy, eatin' her heart out and loving you so much, she was dyin' inside." He shoved his plate aside. "And you. You're worse."

Bart pushed his own plate back. "She didn't love me," he muttered. "It was all just a game for her. All of this. Living here. Me. Everything. It was just some game she was playing."

The older man snorted derisively. "And you weren't playin' no games?"

"No, I wasn't," Bart declared angrily.

"Seems to me you're living by some kinda double standard," Bill said.

"Meaning?" Bart demanded. But he knew what the older man meant.

Bill stood and began clearing the table. "I admit I disapprove of her livin' with you like she did," he said as he worked. "And I told her so. Told her it was wrong. I told her you weren't an honorable man." He chuckled, remembering how her eyes had flashed. "Made her pretty mad, that did. Didn't defend herself, just you."

"She defended me?" Bart asked. He had called her selfish. He had accused her of not caring, and she had been defending him to Bill Andrews. His sweet witch had been standing up for him, rather than worrying about herself or what Bill had thought of her.

"Yep. Told me you were very honorable. Told me you hadn't made her no promises." Bill shook his head. "You two were fools. No promises. Love is all the promise anyone ever needs."

"I asked her to stay," Bart said, trying to defend himself.

"Girl was only here for a month 'cause a the house," Bill said. "She couldn't up and stay, and you know it. Specially when you pretended you didn't ever want to work again and didn't care about the future. You was safe and you know it. Missy couldn't blindly agree to something like that."

Bart didn't answer. What could he say? Everything the older man had said was true. He had played a game with her.

"Bart, if you love that girl, it'll last anywhere, not just here."

"I know that." He sighed and sat down at the table again, sipping at the strong coffee.

"Then prove it to her," Bill urged.

"How?"

"Son, you ain't stupid."

Bart pushed his coffee cup aside roughly, almost knocking it over and stood, stepping on Thoth's tail. The cat yowled and fled to a corner. "What am I supposed to do?" he demanded. "Am I supposed to chase her down and beg?"

Bill grinned. "Yep. And you ain't supposed to stop chasing her for the next hundred years." He winked. "I'll tell you a little secret, man to man. You chase her right, son, and you won't never have to beg."


"Thank heavens. It's happened at last."

Andrea glanced up from the file as Julie sank into a chair by her desk.

"What's happened at last?"

"You've come out of mourning," Julie said.

"Julie, I know I've been a little down, but I haven't been that bad."

"You've even worn black jeans and black sweatshirts. Don't tell me you haven't been that bad. I'm surprised you didn't wear black to my wedding."

"I couldn't." Andrea laughed. "You had picked my dress." Andrea looked at herself. The somber navy blue didn't seem much better than black. "I have been pretty grim, haven't I."

"Not grim, morbid." Julie leaned forward in the chair. "I wish you'd talk about it. It might help."

Andrea shook her head. "Maybe in a year or two. In the meantime, what night are you and David free? I was thinking about making some lasagna."

"Sounds wonderful." Julie sighed.

"Don't tell me you're already tired of cooking and cleaning." Andrea grinned mischievously. "Wasn't it you who said someday I'd meet someone and not care if that's all I did?" Julie had been right about that. She would much rather be cooking and cleaning for Bart Collins than running an accounting firm or planning a dinner for friends.

"Thinking dinner with you sounds wonderful has nothing to do with being tired of domesticity," Julie said. "It means I'm glad you're considering joining the world again. Speaking of which, David's bringing Jim for dinner tonight. Why don't you join us?"

Andrea shook her head. "No, thank you, Julie."

It took a lot longer to fall out of love than in. It would still be a long time before she was ready to even think about another relationship, no matter how superficial. And she certainly wasn't ready for an evening of social flirting, which Jim would expect.

"Andrea, you haven't been out in weeks."

"I'm enjoying my solitude. I've needed the time to do some thinking."

Julie sighed again. "You've changed a lot, you know."

"I know." Andrea smiled. She had. She no longer felt compelled to go to the spa, to play tennis every weekend or attend half the events she'd looked forward to attending before. "Not all for the bad, I hope."

"No, not bad, just different," Julie said, standing. "Is your mother still mad?"

"Mom doesn't change." Now it was Andrea's turn to sigh. Tina had been so angry over her decision to keep the house that she had enlisted Julie's and even David's help to convince her how irresponsible she was being. "And she doesn't like it when one of us goes against what she feels is sensible."

"You aren't having as much to do with your family as you used to."

Andrea shrugged. She didn't spend as many evenings with them, but she was no less involved in their lives. She conscientiously met their needs just as she always had, even when they felt unreasonably demanding. She might be more selfish with her time, but she wasn't going to neglect her responsibilities.

"Amanda and Rory are grown. Amanda's getting married in a week, and Rory has his office open now. They don't need me to hold their hands anymore, and I need some time of my own. I still have a lot of thinking to do."

"It might help if you'd talk about him."

She wished she could, but Bart Collins was too special, too personal to share, even with Julie. As usual she turned her reply into a teasing question.

"You're so sure there is a him?"

"As sure as I can be without a little validation from you or having met him."

It was obvious to Andrea that Julie was no longer sure that there was a "him." She knew her friend assumed it the most likely cause of her recent withdrawal and depressed mood. It was the easiest explanation, but her repeated denials and refusal to talk had begun to deflect Julie's suspicions at last.

"Well, I'm off." Julie stood, stretching. "Don't work too late. Save some strength for April."

"I'll just finish up this file. I won't be long." Julie started for the door. "Julie, thanks for not prying."

Julie smiled. "I would, if it would do any good. And if the man was around, I'd wring his neck for hurting you."

Andrea smiled back. "No, you wouldn't. You'd go into matchmaking overdrive."

Julie waved and disappeared down the hall, and Andrea turned back to the folders still on her desk. The work held no interest. Swiveling her chair, she gazed out the window into the early evening. Wringing his neck wasn't exactly what she would do, but it was close. It was her own neck that should be wrung.

She had known full well what she was doing. She had known it was a fling, a vacation affair, an enchanted interlude. She had stupidly thought she could do it. Bart Collins was the mistake she would have to learn to live with.

# Eight

Bart was just reaching for the door when it was pulled open by a pretty brunette. The woman glanced up, gasped and stepped back. Bart also took a step back, realizing he had startled her in the half-light.

"I'm sorry, I didn't mean to startle you. I was looking for Andrea MacLarson. Is she here?"

"I'm sorry, we've closed for the day. Did you have an appointment with Miss MacLarson?"

She sounded much like Andrea had the day she reprimanded him about the dogs—firm and just a little uncertain. "No, I didn't. You must be Julie Costley." Belatedly Bart remembered Julie's marriage. "Congratulations on your marriage. Andrea never mentioned your fiancé's last name. She just called him David."

"Walker," Julie answered automatically. "Are you a friend of Andrea's?"

"Yes. I just got in and was hoping to catch her before she left." He glanced at his watch. "The plane was delayed in Atlanta. What time do you open in the morning?"

Bart was unaware that his disappointment was almost palpable. Julie glanced from him to the two suitcases at his feet. "You came straight from the airport?"

"Yes." Bart glanced at the quiet street behind him. "Could I use your phone to call a cab? And could you suggest a hotel?"

"Could I ask you one question first?" Bart nodded. "Where did you meet Andrea?"

"In New Mexico."

"Then I'll do even better than letting you use the phone. Andrea's still here." Julie smiled and opened the door. "If you'll follow me, please."

He entered the office, setting his bags in the reception area before following the brunette down a dimly lighted hallway to the second door on the right. Light spilled through the doorway, pooling in a square puddle. Bart stopped at the edge of the pool and hesitated as one would before stepping into a rushing stream. She was sitting with her back to the door, staring out the window, her head propped on one hand.

"Andrea," Julie said. "I've changed my mind."

Andrea turned, closing the folder and neatly stacking several files. She wasn't going to get any more work done today. She might as well walk out with Julie. "About what?"

"This." Julie gestured to Bart to come in.

Slowly Bart stepped into the room, pausing just inside the door. His heart had never beaten this hard or his knees felt so weak in his entire life. His eyes met Andrea's. "Hello, Gypsy."

Andrea felt every muscle in her body freeze, then tremble violently. It wasn't a dream. Or if it was, it was a very vivid hallucination. "Mr. Collins?"

"Yes, Gypsy." He took another step into the room. "How are you?"

Numb, she thought, absolutely numb.

Bart wanted to cross the room, round the desk and take her into his arms, to hold her and reassure her. She looked stunned until Julie spoke again. He realized it was girl talk, but it upset Gypsy, flushing her face and making her look away for a moment.

"Gypsy?" Julie glanced from Bart to Andrea and back. "Someday you're going to have to do some explaining, Andrea. But I love it." She sighed, sounding much more like an enrapt teen than a thirty-year-old, married woman. "I wasn't wrong, after all. Was I, Andrea?"

Andrea looked at Bart, still not believing that he was standing in her office. "No," she whispered, feeling her face flush, knowing Julie's mind would jump to all sorts of conclusions, most of them fairly accurate. No, Julie hadn't been wrong. There had been a man, and now he was standing in her office, looking at her with those wonderful, brown eyes and speaking to her in that lovely, deep voice. She didn't know whether to wring his neck or throw herself into his arms.

"I'll be darned." Julie seemed to realize how inappropriate her behavior was. "Well, I'll be going. I'm sure you two have a lot of talking to do. Good night."

"Julie." Andrea wasn't ready to be alone with him. She heard the front door click shut in the silence and wondered why she hadn't heard the voices earlier. She swallowed, unable to take her eyes off the towering figure that filled her office. He looked so good, so strong and tall. She could throw herself into his arms and he would hold her, still her trembling. He hadn't changed, but it had only been ten weeks. No, he looked tense, a little wary, as if she would attack or bite. Maybe she should.

"Why?" Was that trembling, hesitant whisper her voice?

"I wanted to see you again. No, I needed to see you. I've missed you, Gypsy. Life isn't the same without you."

"I've—" Andrea mentally shook herself. It had taken her weeks to get to the point where she could function without the agonizing pain that loving him had caused. She couldn't, she wouldn't go through that again. Slowly she stood, not sure her legs would hold her, but needing to be on more equal footing.

"No. It's over." At least her voice sounded firm and in control, even though she knew she wasn't.

"Is it, Gypsy? Is it really over?"

No. It never would be over for her. Ten, fifty years from now her reaction would be just as sharp, her memories just as fresh. "Yes!"

It was the anguish in her voice that sent him around the desk. It was the pain printed so starkly on her face that held him just inches from her. "You said we made no promises." She nodded in agreement. "We did," he said softly. She shook her head. "What we shared was a commitment. What happened between us was not a vacation affair." Bart reached out to gently trace the curve of her cheek. "I'm here to show you that."

Fire streaked through her at his gentle touch. She fought the natural urge of her body as her senses were overwhelmed. He had brought the smell of the forest with him, the clean scent of male. She stiffened her spine, clutching the edge of the desk for support, and glared at him.

"It wasn't a promise, Bart. It wasn't. And it's past. It's over." That wonderful sharing of time and interests had not been a part of the present or the future. She had known it then, just as she knew it now. "What we had was then. It's not part of my future."

Bart smiled with understanding. It had taken him nine weeks to face the truth. If she still feared commitment more than solitude, he would just have to prove to her that it could be what they both wanted.

"It can be, Gypsy, if that's what we both want."

"It's not what I want," she said knowing she lied. "And don't you think it would be best not to use that ridiculous name?"

Bart laughed softly. "It isn't a ridiculous name at all, sweet witch. Sometimes it is very difficult to separate fantasy and reality and know which is which."

"And you know the difference?" she demanded. He hadn't known the difference before. If he had, he would have understood that she'd had to return.

"It took me a while to figure it out," he admitted, his eyes resting on her face. "But I had the help of a gypsy, a magical mountain and a very wise old man." Bart smiled, his eyes sweeping from the tightly pinned hair over the severe lines of the dark suit she wore. "Now it's time for you to learn the difference."

"I know the difference," Andrea said firmly.

"No you don't, not yet."

"And you plan to teach me, I suppose."

Bart grinned. "Yes, I certainly do, starting with dinner."

Andrea glared at him, opened her mouth to speak—and stopped as the phone shrilled. "Yes," she snapped into the receiver. Her eyes switched to Bart and then back to the phone.

"You certainly did," she said, "but we'll discuss that tomorrow." She listened again and then sighed and spoke more gently. "No, I'm not." Slowly she replaced the phone and turned back to face Bart Collins.

"I'm glad you aren't angry with Julie," Bart said.

"I'm furious with Julie," she retorted.

"You told her you weren't."

"I told her I wasn't in any physical danger."

"Aren't you?" Bart teased, letting his eyes drink in every inch of her lovely, slender body.

She looked much as she had the day she had appeared on his doorstep to get the cats. Her hair was pinned in a neat chignon. She was dressed in a tailored business suit, her legs shimmered in silk hose. Only she was thinner. She had lost weight she couldn't afford to lose, and there were dark smudges under her eyes.

His heart ached, knowing the pain he had caused her. He wanted to take her into his arms and promise her he would never hurt her again. But it was too soon. She wouldn't believe him now. Slowly she moistened her lips, the tip of her tongue teasing against her lower lip.

"You are definitely in physical danger if you do that again," Bart promised, barely able to refrain from embracing her and tasting those sweet lips. He wanted to pull the pins from her hair, and hold her. He wanted to strip the suit from her body and take her, here, now.

"Do what?"

Her words came out in a trembling whisper. His blatant appraisal had left her shaking with desire—and with fear that she wouldn't be strong enough to resist the temptation.

Bart reached out and lightly touched her lip. "That," he said, lightly following the same path her tongue had taken. "Now get your purse, turn off the lights, and let's go have some dinner."

"I've got work to do."

"Do you really think you'll be able to work tonight?"

"Yes," she said, aware that she lied again.

Bart chuckled. "I thought you said you knew the difference between fantasy and reality, Gypsy."

"Damn you, Bart Collins. I've got a business to run and work to do. I don't have time to play games with you."

"I'm not going to interfere in your business or your work." He reached across the desk and flicked off the desk lamp. "Nor am I here to play games."

How could she possibly concentrate, knowing he was around, knowing he was waiting for her in the evenings? "You're already interfering. I need to be working now." It didn't matter whether he stayed or went—he'd break into her thoughts by day, her dreams by night.

"You need dinner and then a night's rest, so you're fresh for tomorrow," Bart said. "Where's your purse?" He began opening drawers, finding the object of his pursuit in the one at the bottom. "Did you wear a coat?"

"Bart."

Straightening, he looked directly into her eyes. "I'm serious, Andrea. It's not a game when I follow a woman fourteen hundred miles across the country." He grinned as he literally pushed her toward the door. "You're so pretty when you're mad. Did I ever tell you that?"

"You told me lots of things, Bart. And you left out just as many."

"Where would you like to go for dinner?"

"Big Burger. The drive-thru window."

Andrea stood in the middle of her living room, staring at the bag of fast food. Bart had taken her to Big Burger, ordered hamburgers at the drive-thru and brought her home. But somehow she had agreed to his suggestion that he borrow her car for the night and pick her up in the morning.

It had been purely self-defense, she assured herself as she began to eat. The sooner she was away from him, the sooner she could think rationally. She didn't want to talk with him, to hear him. So, if letting him borrow the car for the night had meant she escaped, it was better. By morning she would have herself under control and be able to deal with him. Yes. In the morning she would be cool and collected and able to deal with Bart Collins, past, present and future.

She had just stepped out of the shower when the doorbell rang. Tugging her terry robe on and trying to wrap a towel around her dripping hair at the same time, she made it to the living room before the bell rang again. Giving up on her hair, she got the robe belted just as it rang for the third time.

"I'm coming," she called, impatiently struggling with the lock.

She didn't feel the cold air that swirled around her feet or chilled her wet hair. She felt on fire from the caress of dark brown eyes. Struggling for the calm control she had promised herself, she spoke again.

"I said seven, Bart. It's barely six."

Instead of being calm and controlled, she sounded rather desperate. But how was she to maintain a placid attitude, when she was still half-asleep and not ready to deal with the world, and he was obviously wide-awake and ready to face the day?

"Good morning, Gypsy," he said, gently forcing the door open and stepping past her. "I'm glad to see you still hate mornings. I'll just have some coffee while you dress."

"I haven't made any."

"I came equipped," he said, gesturing to the large grocery bag in his hand.

Andrea gave up and closed the door. She never had known how to get rid of him. "The kitchen's through there." He turned away. "Bart, this is the last time."

"We'll see, Gypsy, we'll see."

Andrea stomped into her bedroom and slammed the door. The man was insufferable. Everything was a game to him, everything. He didn't take anything in life seriously, not a thing. Not even her. Last night he had said his being here wasn't a game. If that was true, he should have arrived at seven, as she'd asked. She pulled on her panties and bra, a slip and her hose as she ranted to herself. She was just slipping into her dress when the door opened.

"Some things haven't changed, have they?" he said as he set a cup of coffee on the dresser.

"No, they haven't. You're still rude and inconsiderate."

"And you still wear too many clothes." Bart stepped behind her and slowly pulled the zipper up, taking forever to complete the task and letting his hands rest far too long on her shoulders. "Breakfast will be ready in ten minutes."

She wanted nothing more than to lean back against him, to let him undo the zipper he had just closed. "I don't eat breakfast."

"You can't work and use that enchanting head of yours if you don't give your body some fuel. Ten minutes."

Something solid hit the door just as he closed it. Bart chuckled and went back to the kitchen to finish preparing the meal.

Andrea glared at the door a full minute before turning back to the dresser and picking up her brush. She pulled it through her hair with a vengeance for several strokes, then paused and looked at the door thoughtfully.

She knew what Bart Collins was. He was a man who had decided he didn't want responsibilities and demands. He was a dreamer who wanted sunsets and picnics, a man who lived for the moment while he searched for life. Her temper tantrums and anger would get her exactly nowhere.

More gently she continued brushing her hair, pinning it into the usual chignon. No, the best course of action would be to let him play his game, let him see her real life. Once he saw she wasn't going to run off and ignore her responsibilities, he would tire of it all and go on. She only had to be calm and reasonable for a couple of weeks.

* * *

Being calm and reasonable was going to be far more difficult than she had thought, Andrea realized an hour later.
Bart she could handle. Julie she could handle. Her mother
she could handle. One at a time. Not all together.

Bart got her to the office on time, despite insisting she eat
breakfast. Her was mother was waiting at the door, toe
tapping impatiently. Since Bart had driven and still had her
keys in his hand, Andrea was forced to make introduc-
tions.

"Hi, Mom. I'd like you to meet Bart Collins. He was one
of my neighbors in New Mexico. Bart, my mother, Tina
MacLarson."

"Good morning, Mrs. MacLarson."

Tina glanced from the keys to Andrea to Bart and then
back to Andrea, giving her a look that said, "We'll talk
later, but not much later."

"Mr. Collins," she said coldly.

Bart sorted through the keys, unlocked the door and held
it for the two women. Andrea's mother brushed by him with
her head high, as if he had insulted her. Andrea's shoulders
were tense, and the glance she gave him was one of a cor-
nered animal. The moment they were inside, Tina Mac-
Larson turned toward him.

"How long do you plan to be in Columbus?"

"My plans aren't definite at the moment, Mrs. Mac-
Larson."

She was nothing like her daughter. She was short and her
figure was full, almost voluptuous. Her coloring was darker,
her hair a dark brown. He could find nothing about them
that suggested they were mother and daughter.

"Are you here on business?"

"Yes." The desperate look on Andrea's face kept him
from saying more, but it didn't keep the older woman from
asking.

"What business are you in?"

Did she give all the men Andrea met this third degree? Or
was it because he was in her daughter's car this early in the

morning? "My business in Columbus is of a personal nature."

"I see."

Tina turned her back, dismissing him with the icy tone. No, but I'm beginning to, Bart thought. He had to grit his teeth to keep from demanding what the woman thought she saw. Only the desperation on Andrea's face convinced him to remain silent as the older woman addressed her daughter.

"Andrea, I need your help. The bridesmaids' dresses weren't shipped with Amanda's gown. You'll have to go to Atlanta and pick them up."

"Sure, Mom." She couldn't quite cover the sigh. She would be so glad when this wedding was over and done with. "When?"

"Today. This morning."

"Today? I can't, Mom, not today."

"Those dresses have to be here today, if the final fittings are to be done on time."

"Mom, I've got a full schedule of appointments this morning. I can clear my calendar for tomorrow with no trouble." It wasn't exactly true that it would be no trouble, but she would rearrange her schedule somehow.

"It's got to be today," Tina said flatly. "Julie can handle the office. You certainly had no qualms about letting her do it while you went off to play in New Mexico."

No qualms, Bart thought, remembering the daily phone calls, the times she had worried about being unfair to Julie. This woman had no idea who her daughter was. No wonder the daughter was so confused.

"Good morning, Mrs. MacLarson, Bart." Andrea turned as Julie spoke. One look at Julie's face told her that she had heard enough of the conversation to know what was happening. "Andrea, I can cover some of your appointments. We'll just have to reschedule the others."

"I knew you'd understand, Julie." Tina smiled, giving Julie an approving look. "I'm going to be late for work if I don't hurry. Drive carefully, Andrea."

"Damn," Andrea muttered as the door closed, then threw her purse onto a chair. "Julie, if you can cover the earliest appointments, Sue can reschedule the rest—at the client's convenience. I don't care—"

"Good morning, Julie." Bart interrupted Andrea's plans, put his arm around her and pulled her close to his side. She was tense and trembling. "Gypsy, if you'll give me the information, I'll go pick up the dresses."

"What about your personal business?" She knew her response was sarcastic. He was only trying to help. But she couldn't deal with all three of these people at once. No, it was his arm around her, the nearness of him that she couldn't cope with. All she wanted to do was lean against him, but Bart Collins didn't want people leaning on him.

"I did have lunch plans," Bart said with a smile. "But I'm sure the person will understand."

Andrea felt the blaze of what could only be called jealousy as Julie told him how grateful they would be for his help. Whom had he planned to have lunch with? Whom else did he know in Columbus?

"Gypsy, if you could drive me to the rental agency so I can pick up my car, I'll be on my way."

She glanced at him and shrugged. "Just use my car." She didn't have time to drive him around or stop for lunch, but she was dying to know whom Bart had planned to see. She and Julie conferred a moment on the best directions. She wrote down all the details he needed on a piece of stationery and handed it to him. Bart headed for the door, but paused.

"Julie, would you do me a favor?"

And now he was asking Julie for favors? Andrea wanted to choke him. She had no idea she could feel this possessive.

"If I can," Julie said.

"See that my lunch date eats. She thinks chocolate-covered peanuts are enough."

Andrea felt her face heat with the blush. She had to fight the urge to throw something.

"I promise," Julie said, laughing at Andrea's expression. "You better hurry, before we have to replace the glass in the door." Bart left, chuckling. "He's wonderful, Andrea. Where did you find him?"

"Under a rock," she muttered.

"Well, that's one rock I'd keep. Did you have a good time last night?"

"I loaned him my car and sent him to a hotel."

"Wow! This is serious!"

Andrea glared at Julie. "Sending him to a hotel is serious?"

"No. But if his just being in town is enough to get you out of all those dark colors, I can't wait to see what you do when things heat up."

Andrea looked down, surprised to find she had dressed in bright green. She knew she as in trouble then.

By that evening she had decided she never wanted to face another day like this one. Bart had come back with the dresses and she had taken enough time to drop them off, call her mother and take Bart to the rental agency to pick up his car. She had calmly refused his near demand to have dinner and returned to the office—only to learn that the computers had gone down.

By the time she got home at eight, she wanted nothing more than to crawl into bed and pull the blankets over her head. She had barely gotten her shoes off when the doorbell rang. She knew it was one of two people, and she couldn't decide whom she wanted to see the least. It was Bart, and he had two take-out dinners.

"Bart, I'm tired. It's been a terribly difficult day." And he was a lot of the difficulty.

"I got liver smothered in onions. They didn't have spinach, so I substituted broccoli."

Andrea looked from him to the boxes and back. "You got me liver?" How could she stay angry, when he had done something so sweet? How could she have treated him so coldly, when he had literally saved the day by going to Atlanta? She stepped back so he could enter. "I'm sorry, Mr. Collins."

"For what?" Bart pushed the door shut with his elbow, watching the emotions flit across her face.

"For snapping at you every time you got within ten feet. Thank you for driving to Atlanta for me."

"You're welcome." Bart headed for the kitchen. One thing he had already learned about his witch was that she could and would become quite waspish when she was upset or felt out of control. He could handle a few stings, while she sorted through things.

"What about a glass of wine before we eat? We can heat this up in the microwave, if it gets cold."

The cats appeared, twining in and out of Bart's legs as Andrea got the glasses. Thoth began to mew, as if he had been the most lonesome thing on the earth. Bart knelt by the animals, petting and talking to them.

"I think they missed you," Andrea said.

"I hope they aren't the only ones."

Andrea wasn't ready to get into that. She picked up the glasses and carried them to the living room. She didn't want to snap and snarl, but she wasn't ready for any personal talk, either. Neutral subjects were the most she could handle and stay calm.

Sticking to neutral subjects was a lot more difficult than Andrea had imagined. Once she learned he had spent the holidays with his family and sold his condominium in New York, the only questions left were the personal ones; the how, what and why of themselves. And the memories.

As the conversation dwindled and died, Andrea suggested they eat. Then she would claim fatigue and thank him. They reheated the food and shared the meal, quietly.

Bart was willing to give Andrea the time and space she needed to adjust to his presence. But once he had questioned her about her sister's wedding and her brother's new veterinary office, he ran out of small talk. He wanted to know how she had been, what she had thought, which memories were the most precious.

After having seen what her day's routine entailed, he might even need some time and space, he admitted. He was the outsider here, the intruder. Outside influences could affect a relationship, and Andrea obviously had outside influences now. He was curious to see her life and get to know the people who had molded this sweet, feisty, shy, sexy woman who had come to mean so much to him.

Andrea was both pleased and disappointed when Bart said it was late and he would go. He hadn't even touched her, hadn't even tried. He made no move to kiss her, not even to hold her hand.

"I'd like to have dinner with you one evening," he said at the door.

Andrea shook her head. "The rest of the week is impossible. Every evening is tied up with Amanda's wedding." She sighed, wishing it was over, then looked up. "Would you like to attend? I realize you don't know anyone involved, but you're welcome to come." If he was still here.

"I know you," Bart said, trying to visualize his gypsy in one of those pink, beribboned things he had picked up earlier. He couldn't.

"I'm involved behind the scenes," Andrea said. "I get to worry about the food and music and cake and dresses."

"I'd love to come," Bart said. "You will have time for at least one dance at the reception?"

"I can probably squeeze one in. If we don't have any last-minute crisis."

"If you do, I'll help you unravel the crisis. And Gypsy, if you need errands run or an extra pair of hands, please tell me."

Tears misted her eyes at his offer. They were due to being tired and the emotional turmoil, she assured herself, not to the fact that someone was offering to take some of the weight from her shoulders. Andrea didn't mind helping with the wedding, but few days were left to her to perform every last function. Amanda wanted a large, formal ceremony, yet she had rushed everything, not leaving enough time to accomplish it all. And it was in the middle of an increasing work load for Andrea.

If Bart had thought his life in New York a rat race, he couldn't begin to define Andrea's. Over the next four days he watched in amazement as she juggled a thriving business, her family and friends and put together a large wedding. Her days were long, hard and exhausting.

He knew tax season had increased her business, yet he realized quickly she had a large number of thriving accounts that would keep her busy year-round. She might be young, but she was very successful. Though Julie was active and carried her share, it was Andrea who was the driving force. Her quick mind and long hours had built the little firm into a major business in a few short years.

Though she didn't call him and ask, she never refused his help, smiling at him in such a way that he would have moved a mountain if she had needed it. By the end of his first week in town, he decided she did need just that, the mountain being her family.

Andrea had spoken of responsibility and duty frequently. How she dealt with the constant demands, he wasn't sure. Her mother, sister and brother all turned to her with every small problem, no matter what time of the day or night.

Frequently he saw flashes of irritation or frustration, but she always covered them and met their needs, too often at her own expense. She skipped lunch to run an errand for her mother, let her supper get cold when Amanda called in tears, dropped her own business needs to help her brother with his accounts. And she added hours to her day, handling the details of the wedding.

Often he wondered if she had a life of her own, or if it was a way of holding him at bay. But he stopped the thoughts, reminding himself that a wedding was an extraordinary event, not routine. He also reminded himself that he had come uninvited. He might want her to make time for him, but he was being unreasonable.

He held his thoughts and his temper—until the evening he learned it wasn't only her time and energy they demanded, but her money, as well. It had been Julie, who told him Andrea's car was in the shop and asked him to drive her home. He had been hurt and angry that she still wouldn't ask him for help.

"Why didn't you call me and tell me you needed a ride?" he demanded as they left the office.

"I thought the car would be ready," she said. "I didn't see any need to bother you."

"You don't like asking for help, do you?"

"I didn't know," she said, her voice sharp. "I was on the phone with them when you called, and matchmaker saw an excuse to be sure we would be together."

"Remind me to send Julie some flowers. Without her I don't think I would ever see you."

"Bart, I told you I didn't have time. Have you ever tried to put a wedding together? There are a hundred details to take care of." She grimaced as she remembered several details she had forgotten. "Would you mind detouring by the florist and the bakery, please?"

"More details?"

"Yes." She gave him a tentative smile. "But I did ask."

Bart tagged along while she took care of the "more details." It was amazing how much one could learn by asking casual questions, when the other person had her mind on another subject. As long as the question was asked in a tone of voice that suggested nothing, the answers came, given over a shoulder or with a quick glance.

By the time she had finished at the bakery, he was furious. As they reached her apartment, Bart knew he was too angry to go in. "Do you need a ride in the morning?"

Andrea started at the sharp tone. Now what had she done? she wondered. "Yes, please. If you can."

"And if I can't?"

Andrea frowned. "I'll call Julie or Sue." What had gotten him so upset?

"Why not call your mother? Or Amanda? Your brother?"

"They all have schedules. Mom has to work, and so do Amanda and Rory."

"They certainly feel free to take your time and interrupt your schedules. You haven't had a minute to yourself since I've been here."

Jealous! He was jealous of the time she gave her family. No, not jealous. It was the pressure of the responsibility. "You aren't obliged to hang around, Bart. You're free to go whenever you like."

"So are you, Andrea. You just don't seem to realize you have the right to say no."

"I don't want to say no. That's where you and I differ. Yes, I have responsibilities, but I don't resent them."

"You should," Bart muttered as she slammed the car door. He followed her to the entrance.

"You have parents and a sister. Are you saying you wouldn't help them if they needed it?"

"Of course I'd help them," Bart snapped.

"Then why is it so wrong for me to help mine?"

"Because you aren't helping them, Andrea. You're taking care of them. Why are you paying for your sister's marriage? And giving your brother free accounting services?"

"Families stick together. Amanda can't afford to pay for this wedding. She just finished college last year. And Rory has just finished, too. It'd be pretty mean not to help him with the books."

"It would be mean not to give him a major discount and extra help. It would be mean not to give your time and energy to your sister. It would be sensible to keep the money for yourself. If you weren't paying for this elaborate wedding and handing out free services, you could afford to have your own place and a little room, rather than living in this tiny apartment. Or you could put the money into a car that was fit to be driving."

"That's funny," Andrea said, but she wasn't laughing. "That's really funny. The last time I got this lecture, I was told if I sold that shack in New Mexico, I would have enough for those things. I don't know why it hasn't occurred to anyone that maybe I don't want to own a condominium or a new car. My God, all I'd have then was more responsibility, higher taxes, higher insurance and more work."

"You don't have responsibilities, Andrea. You're being taken advantage of, and you're too blind to see it."

# Nine

Andrea slammed the door at his words, tears burning her eyes. "I'm just tired," she muttered as she fed the cats. "Okay, so I didn't need a car repair on top of everything else, but that gives him no right to say the things he did."

No matter how much she wanted to dismiss his words as simply those of someone who didn't care, she couldn't. He was right. If Amanda had just waited until the summer or fall. If Rory hadn't needed the financial help, opening his office. But they had, and unlike her father, she wouldn't walk away just because it was hard. Everything in her life was stretched to the limit; time, energy and money.

Andrea left the cats eating and walked through the dark apartment to the bedroom, dropped her jacket and sank down onto the side of the bed. She had known that if she stayed calm and reasonable, he would begin to get restless. He wasn't at a point in his life where he wanted all the obligations a family meant. She could understand that. It was why she had worked so hard to keep things friendly but neutral.

Mercury jumped onto the bed, settling by her hip, a small spot of warmth in the empty room. Tears burned her eyes with renewed force. She was lonely. All she wanted in the world was to lean her head against Mr. Collins's shoulder and let his strong arms surround her. He might not want all the headaches of a stable life, but she drew strength from him, and tonight she needed that strength.

The hot tears fell at last. Andrea lay back, then turned onto her stomach, burying her face in the spread. When the phone rang, she muttered the worst oath she knew and yanked the cord from the wall.

Bart slammed the cup down hard enough to crack the china. He rarely let his temper show in such ways, preferring to use the energy in a hard workout or running. He had already run miles this morning and doubted another workout would help, unless it happened to be in a certain redhead's bed.

"Fat chance of that," he muttered. "She's got those damned walls so thick, it'd take dynamite to get through to her. Besides, I'd probably no sooner get her on the damned bed than someone would have a crisis and she'd have to go."

He had known she would have demands on her time. He hadn't expected to spend every minute with her, as he had in new Mexico. He had expected to have more than five or ten minutes spent in a car, or brief conversations on the phone that consisted of her telling him how busy she was. He had expected more than take-out food interrupted by phone calls.

Bart sat down on the unmade bed. Maybe he had been wrong. Maybe Bill had been wrong, too. It was highly probable that she really didn't care, that she found his presence an unwanted intrusion. It would explain all the excuses. It would explain why she ignored him and used her family as a reason to avoid him.

He didn't like his train of thought at all, but it made sense. It would certainly explain why she had kept him at arm's length. But it didn't explain what they had had before. He couldn't have been that wrong about her.

A new and equally unpleasant idea rebutted that thought. Bart went back to the table and refilled the cup, surprised to see it hadn't cracked.

Andrea was not the type of woman to give in to a physical attraction, no matter how strong that attraction. And it had been the strongest he had ever known. It was possible she had convinced herself it was more while she was there, an excuse to allow herself to give in to the almost overwhelming desire that had existed between them. Now his presence was making her face the truth. Coming here was probably one of the worst mistakes he had ever made.

His presence was probably causing her guilt. It would explain the obvious discomfort she felt around him, not passion denied but simple embarrassment. He finished the coffee with a grimace. He had been selfish in coming here, in listening to an old man's ravings because that was what he had wanted to hear. If she had wanted him to come, she would have gotten in touch with him. She could have contacted his old office in New York, or even Bill.

Glancing at the clock, he began dressing. Mistake or not, he had promised her a ride this morning. And sometime today, or maybe tomorrow after the wedding, he would apologize and be on his way. Where he didn't know. He had never felt so directionless in his life. Just as he pulled a shirt from the closet, there was a knock at the door.

Andrea knew exactly what she was going to say—until he opened the door. When she saw him, his broad chest and shoulders bare, inviting touch, she did what she had wanted to do for days. She walked straight into his open arms, even if they were open only to hold the door, slipped her own arms around him and leaned her cheek against his shoulder.

Andrea sighed as his heat warmed her, his strength supported her. The fresh, clean, male scent of his body enveloped her. All this time had been wasted, when she could have been right where she needed to be. All this time had been spent worrying about responsibility and duty, trying to prove that she was reliable.

All she had proved was that she was lonely. She wasn't dependent on him. She didn't even want the added responsibility of marriage, so why did she feel it so necessary to demand these qualities from him?

Bart was stunned. He would have sworn the last thing to happen would be for her to show up at his hotel. When she walked straight to him and wrapped her arms around him, leaning against him with a sigh, he knew it was the last thing he'd expected.

He pushed the door shut and put his arms about her, pulling her close, resting his cheek on her neatly pinned hair. Her coat still held the chill of the outdoors, contrasting sharply with the heat of his own body. All the desire and need he had suppressed came to life with renewed force.

Slowly she moved her head from beneath his, tipping hers back to look up at him. Her eyes were sad and uncertain, the lids puffy, as if she had been crying. "Mr. Collins, would you accept one more apology?"

"For what?"

"For trying to pretend you were merely a friend. For holding you away and putting everything else ahead of you."

He hadn't meant to make her feel guilty or responsible for him. That had not been the purpose of his sharp words last night. "I'm sorry for coming uninvited, when you have more than you can handle. I didn't mean to make things more difficult."

"I think I'm doing that all by myself." Andrea sighed, leaning into him again. "Would you hold me, please?"

Bart hesitated a long moment before answering her. Her clothes and the thick coat she wore kept her from realizing how desperately he wanted and needed her. He kept his voice gentle but firm, even and calm—he hoped. "No, Gypsy. I don't have that much willpower."

Andrea held very still, only then realizing how rapidly his heart was beating beneath her ear, his breathing not quite steady. Even his muscles had a slight tremor beneath her hands. "I don't have that much willpower, either," she admitted.

"Do you still want me to hold you?" His question was a hoarse whisper, his voice barely functioning.

"Yes." She sighed again, as if the weight of the world were on her shoulders. "But later. I need to go to work."

"Oh, no, little witch," Bart said. "The office doesn't open until nine. You don't have your first appointment until nine-thirty. I plan to hold you now."

Andrea looked at his watch. "That doesn't give me much time."

"It's a start," he promised. "Just a start. Tonight I plan to make up for anything I miss this morning."

"Tonight's the rehearsal and dinner."

"Gypsy! Yes or no."

She didn't answer. She just began unbuttoning her coat, her face flushed, her eyes soft and misty.

"Let me," he said, brushing her hands aside. Carefully he undressed her, removing each piece of clothing and laying it aside neatly.

Andrea had never known that getting undressed could be torture. He undid each button, hook and snap carefully. He laid her clothes so they would not look rumpled. He didn't touch her. He didn't let his fingers linger or brush against her skin.

If it hadn't been for the tension she saw on his face, she would have thought the task was having no effect on him. But his muscles were strained with holding back, his eyes hot, touching where he didn't allow his hands to go. Her skin burned with the torment. When she stood before him, aching with need, he turned her around and began removing the pins from her hair, one at a time.

Only when her hair was free of all its pins did he turn her back to face him. Andrea seriously thought about attacking him as he stripped off his slacks. She didn't have time to waste. She had already wasted days. Her body was on fire, hot and aching with a need only he could satisfy. He couldn't hide his need. It was boldly evident, the only thing that kept her still and waiting.

He stepped back, his eyes holding hers as he opened his arms. "Let me hold you, Gypsy."

"Oh, yes." She walked into his embrace, meeting him thigh to thigh, belly to belly, breast to chest. His arms closed around her, molding her even closer to the heat of his body, the firm skin and hard muscle. His hands skimmed the contour of her back and buttocks, his long fingers delving into the heart of her femininity.

"Yes," he growled, easing her onto the bed, following her down and entering her in one fluid motion.

Andrea sucked in her breath as he filled her, then let it out on a slow sigh of pure contentment. This was what she had needed, wanted. This was why her life had been so empty. She slipped her arms around him, holding him tightly, complete.

It seemed they lay that way for a long time, savoring each nuance. Andrea reveled in the warmth and strength and tenderness of the man holding her, filling her. She became intoxicated by his scent. Bart marveled at the wonder of being held prisoner by her velvet sheath, by the slender arms and legs that chained him with tender strength. Her scent, like a warm, springtime meadow, made his head spin.

But it wasn't enough. She wanted to touch, to feel the iron-hard muscle beneath the warm skin. She wanted to taste, to explore. She wanted to feel the heat of his lips against her breasts, his silken hair against her fingers.

Before she moved or signaled this new need he was there, cupping her face in his hands, his lips meeting hers, drinking hungrily, just as she did. Their tongues met, parted and tangled in a sweet love play. All patience was lost as raw need took over, desire demanding response. They parted and met, the rhythm fast, taking, demanding and giving. If what they had shared before had been shattering, this was a cataclysm, shaking the very foundation of her being. Andrea lay in his arms, at peace for the first time in three months.

Bart opened one eye far enough to see the time. The last thing in the world he wanted was to leave her trembling arms, her soft, welcoming body. She had been fire beneath him, responding to each move almost before he knew he was going to make it. His own body still felt weak from the impact.

"Gypsy, you're going to have to get dressed. It's quarter till."

She groaned, snuggling closer to him. "I don't have the strength to dress, Mr. Collins."

"You're out of shape if that's all it took to wear you out."

"I thought you liked my shape."

Bart growled softly, nipping at her shoulder. "I do. I like it so much that if you aren't off this bed and into some clothes by the count of ten, you won't get a chance to leave this bed until next week."

The idea sounded so tempting. But today was full, and the rehearsal was tonight. As much as she wanted to tease him, she couldn't. She jumped up as he reached four, grabbing his shirt for a cover.

"May I use your shower?"

Bart nodded, a smile twitching at the corners of his mouth. "Want me to join you?"

"If you do that, I won't make it to work."

Bart chuckled as she dashed into the bathroom. She was right about that. He pushed himself off the bed and began to drag on his own clothes. Tonight, when she finished with work and the wedding problems, he would make sure they had some time alone, even if he had to kidnap her. Time without phone calls or interruptions, just like this morning.

Bart glanced at the room. It was the perfect idea but not the perfect room. For just himself the room was fine, but he couldn't, he wouldn't ask her to eat in front of the bed. It wasn't very romantic. Today he would get a suite. Then they could sit and talk or have a quiet meal without giving their meeting such a clandestine air.

Andrea came out of the bathroom, dressed. She stopped at the mirror and began combing her hair, twisting it to pin up. Bart stepped behind her and caught her wrist.

"Don't. Wear it down."

"I'm going to work. It's not very professional to have hair flying all over the place."

It sounded just like something her mother would say. "Have you ever worn it down?"

"No."

"Try it. If it gets in your way, you can put it up later."

Andrea released her hair, ran the comb through it one more time and shrugged. She could always put it up later, and it really wasn't worth arguing about.

"That's a very pretty color on you," Bart said, holding her coat.

"It's kind of drab," Andrea said. When she had dressed for work the first time, the drab brown had been perfect. Now she wished she had worn fire-engine red or canary yellow.

"Not on you." He turned her to face him. "It brings out all the red in your hair and those little brown flecks in your eyes. You look lovely." She not only looked lovely, she looked well loved. Her cheeks were softly flushed and her lips slightly swollen. "Let's get you to work before they send out the army."

Andrea sat in the back of the church, watching the proceedings. She wasn't sure why she was here—it was just the rehearsal, after all—but she supposed some last-minute glitch could occur, necessitating her intervention.

Tomorrow it would be over. Amanda would be married and on her honeymoon. At least, life in general would begin to return to normal. In the shelter of the darkened pew Andrea scowled toward where her mother was sitting.

She had arrived on time, but her mother had instantly made a remark about her hair being in a mess. And then, as if just noticing Bart, she had dragged Andrea to one side, saying that they hadn't planned on his presence at the dinner. She had spoken in a stage whisper loud enough to carry, so that everyone heard. As if that wasn't bad enough, she then demanded where Andrea had been all night.

Andrea had bitten back the retort that her money was being spent here, and if she wanted Bart present, he would be there. She hadn't bothered to respond to the question about where she had been last night. She had no guilty conscience about last night, when she had unplugged the phone.

Nor did she feel the least uncomfortable about this morning.

So she had replied calmly and clearly, also in a voice meant to be heard, that she and Bart had plans for the evening and would not be staying for the dinner.

Amanda had instantly announced to one of her friends that another person, evidently the girl's boyfriend, could stay, after all. Andrea had turned and calmly told her sister that she had canceled the reservation early enough not to be charged for her place. If the friend wanted to stay, one of them would have to pay. Amanda had burst into tears, her mother had stormed off, sputtering, and Andrea had found a quiet seat at the back of the church.

Bart stood to one side, watching and listening. He was furious with Tina MacLarson, first for saying that Andrea's hair looked like a rat's nest, and then for trying to embarrass him. Probably so that he would leave, he thought, listening as Andrea replied in a calm, clear voice. He smiled, wondering what the woman would say if she knew exactly what his plans for her daughter were.

But when Amanda threw the temper tantrum about have to pay for an extra guest, he couldn't take it. He walked outside and stood in the cold air. He didn't want to embarrass Andrea by watching childish displays of emotion. Nor did he want to alienate her by stepping in and saying exactly what he thought. He didn't understand the dynamics in this family. Andrea was expected—and believed it her duty—to be at their beck and call and make things right for all of them, while her sister was nothing more than a spoiled brat. Her brother fell somewhere in between.

Hearing the first strains of music, he knew the rehearsal had started; the bickering would at least be on hold. Bart returned to the church. It took him a moment to locate Andrea. She wasn't sitting up front but at the back, just a few feet from where he stood. Tension was evident in every line of her body.

He slipped into the pew behind her and leaned forward. "What I would like to know, Miss MacLarson, is where you were last night."

She glanced over her shoulder at him and shrugged. "At home. I unplugged the phone."

She had unplugged the phone. He wondered about the reasons, but didn't push, not now. "What are your plans for tonight?"

"I was promised an uninterrupted, quiet dinner."

"And you'll have it," he said. "I was thinking of after dinner. Are you going home to unplug your phone again?"

"I suppose that depends on whether I get better offers," she said.

"Shall we go to dinner and see what options we can come up with?"

Andrea stood and turned. "Yes."

When he had first mentioned dinner, talking about a quiet spot with no interruptions, Andrea had not thought of his hotel, especially not his room. But as he guided her into the elevator, she admitted that it was probably one of the few places in town where she wouldn't be disturbed. At least the front desk could hold all calls. It might not stop her mother from coming straight to the room, but she doubted even her mother had that much audacity.

She hadn't realized she was disappointed until he got off on a different floor, led her down the corridor to a different room and opened the door. When she saw the small sitting room with the table set for two, she turned into his arms. "Thank you." She didn't have to stare at the bed, knowing what was on both their minds. She could just enjoy her dinner.

"You're welcome." Bart held her for a moment, then helped her with her coat and turned on some music. He called room service and settled on the sofa beside her. "Emotions in your family are running pretty high tonight."

"I guess it's just the wedding and all. Mom is losing her baby, and it was so rushed, getting everything done. It'll be over tomorrow."

"Was Julie's wedding this way?"

"No, it was smaller, for one thing. Julie got frantic a few times, but it was really a lovely affair."

Bart pulled her closer and she leaned her head against his shoulder. He allowed himself the pleasure of running his fingers through her hair, letting the coppery waves flow across his hand. "What kind of wedding do you want?"

Andrea wished she had the courage to look up and try to read his expression. He wasn't suddenly thinking about settling down, was he? No, it had to be a rhetorical remark. "I'd elope."

"I thought you said all women wanted a big wedding the first time."

"I'm not all women," Andrea reminded him. "I don't want to get married. And I sure don't want to spend thousands of dollars and get an ulcer ever again."

"Do you know what you need, little witch?"

"What?"

He felt her tense at his question, as if she was waiting to be criticized. He had to take a deep breath to control his own anger. She was a lovely, caring person who had been misused too long. But he also knew that his next statement was going to make her mad. "You need someone to take care of you."

Andrea smiled, remembering the afternoon he had first said that. He had built a fire, cooked her supper and talked with her. She hadn't wanted to admit it, but she had loved every moment of the attention.

But this was different. Now she was at home, dealing with her job and family. "I am perfectly capable of taking care of myself. Not only am I capable of doing it, I do it. And I do it well."

"Of course you are, and I agree, you do it very well. I'm very impressed with your business and the way you handle things."

"Then why do you say I need someone to take care of me?"

He was saved from trying to explain the difference by the arrival of their dinner. Once the candles were lighted and the food served, she seemed content to enjoy the meal without more words. He refrained from telling her that this was what he meant by taking care of her.

Andrea ate, enjoying the peace and silence. No phones rang. No one knocked on the door. It was pure heaven to sit quietly and enjoy the food and music. It had been weeks since she had had an uninterrupted meal.

"It was delicious," she said with a sigh, laying her fork down at last.

Bart moved the table out of the way. "Do you have plans for the evening?"

The tension was there again, the need and desire, but she wanted to savor the peace. She walked to the sofa and sat down. "Mmm-hmm. I plan to sit here and enjoy this lovely, quiet evening you have given me."

Bart joined her on the sofa. She pulled her feet up and leaned her head against his shoulder, letting one hand rest over the steady beat of his heart. "I needed this."

"I know."

Bart contented himself with stroking her hair and back, feeling the tension slowly ease from her shoulders. She needed a lot of things, he thought. She needed to learn how to make time for herself. She needed to learn how to say no. She needed to learn the difference between accepting responsibility and letting herself be used.

The tension between them increased slowly. The hunger had been tamed this morning, but not satisfied. Bart smiled, his lips against her hair. Their hunger would never be satisfied. It would always be there, fresh and new. Gently he tipped her face up.

"Stay with me tonight, Gypsy."

She nodded, her expression solemn. Bart lifted her into his arms and carried her into the bedroom.

Andrea stretched and settled back against Bart's chest. The sky was just beginning to lighten outside. She had a busy day ahead. First she had to go to the church and make sure the flowers arrived and were placed properly. She had to check on the reception hall and the caterers. There were dozens of little details to worry about. But for a few more minutes she was simply going to enjoy the wonderful pleasure of being next to Mr. Collins.

"Woman, if you wiggle like that one more time, I won't be responsible for my actions."

Andrea's smile was one of pure, feminine satisfaction as she snuggled her back closer to his chest. Bart Collins always made her feel desirable, sensuous and sexy. A large hand skimmed over her hips, splaying itself across her stomach and pressing her even closer to the heat of his body.

"Don't you ever sleep late?" She tried to sound irritated, but it was hard to do when her body was responding to his as it always did.

"I might, if you weren't constantly trying to seduce me."

"If I wanted to seduce you, Mr. Collins, I would."

His sexy chuckle rumbled against her back. "Then what were you trying to do?"

"Get comfortable." She wiggled once more, aware of his aroused state, her own body already softening in anticipation. "And I am."

"Well, I'm not," Bart growled next to her ear.

"Then I'll be very still, so you can get comfortable."

Her heart pounded as Bart shifted slightly, placing one hand over her breast, the other caressing her hip and thigh. He shifted again, pulling away from her only to come back, joining their bodies.

"Now I'm comfortable," he murmured, nibbling on her shoulder. "What are your plans for today?"

Plans? Today? How was she supposed to think of mundane things like flowers and wedding cakes, when Mr. Collins was doing what he was doing to her? She could hardly remember to breathe.

"Don't tell me you have a day with no plans," he teased.

He gently massaged first one breast, then the other, with one hand, while he kept his hand firmly over her stomach, so she couldn't move.

"I can't think about my plans like this," Andrea whispered.

"Like what?"

Each time he spoke his breath fanned across her shoulder, his beard brushed her skin like a feather. She had had no idea her back had so many nerve endings.

"You're torturing me."

"Torturing you?"

"Yes....Uh..." He increased the torture. His lips skimmed over her shoulder and neck. The hand over her breast became more insistent, while he slipped the one over her stomach down into the nest of curls. He found the small nub that sent her already enflamed body bursting into sweet fire. "Mr. Collins."

Her slender body convulsed around his as she called his name. Bart held her, his face buried in the silken tumble of copper waves. Slowly he moved, disengaging their bodies and allowing her to turn onto her back. He stroked the gentle arch of one brow, looking into the depths of her green eyes.

"Good morning, sweet witch."

"Good morning, Mr. Collins."

He traced the shape of her mouth, watching the expression in her eyes change from a soft misty satisfaction to the slow warming of renewed passion. She freed her hands and reached up, sculpting his face, trailing her fingers across his mouth.

Desire and need surged through his body. It was always that way with her. No matter how many times they made love, he was ready for more. He needed her again.

"Mr. Collins."

"Yes, Gypsy?"

"I—"

Other emotions flickered through her eyes. Doubt. Fear. Need. He knew in a deep, instinctive part of his soul that she had almost said, "I love you." He cupped her face in his hands, threading his fingers into her hair. No more able to say the words than she, he showed her, pouring all his feelings into his lovemaking.

Bart had sat silent for the last fifteen minutes, growing angrier with each second that passed. He had watched her race through a quick shower, dress and swallow a cup of coffee, the whole time giving him a verbal list of all the things she had to do.

She was rebuilding the walls. She was telling him he had no part in her life, except at night. Did she really think she could put him into a little category—Great Night of Sex—and continue with the rest of her life as if he weren't there? She wriggled her foot into a shoe, reaching for her purse. Well, she couldn't. He wouldn't let her. She would either let him be a part of her life or not, but he wouldn't be shoved off to one side like this.

"I guess I'll see you at the church later."

She didn't sound very pleased with that idea, either. "Yes. I'll be there."

"Oh, well, I guess I better get busy." Andrea reached for her coat and froze. "Oh, no! Of all the stupid things to do."

Bart listened in surprise as she swore angrily. "What's wrong?"

She turned and looked at him. "I forgot to pick up my car yesterday." Her expression changed from absolute dismay to icy anger. "And you knew it. The whole time I was getting ready, you sat there, drinking your coffee, knowing I didn't have my car."

It's simple, Bart thought. Just let me in. Ask me. Say you need my help. He didn't offer, waiting for her to make the move, to voluntarily open the door for him. Just having her in his bed wasn't going to be enough. He wanted to be a part of her life.

Andrea couldn't believe he would sit there, his expression one of irritation. He was just watching her. She had no idea what he wanted her to do. She had things to attend to, details to take care of, and then she had to dress for the wedding. She knew she didn't have time to worry about Bart Collins. It was her responsibility to be sure that the church was decorated and the reception ran smoothly. Bart Collins didn't understand responsibility. Suddenly, totally unexpectedly, she burst into tears.

Bart had never seen her cry except the night she thought he had left New Mexico without saying goodbye. Even then she had been wet, cold and frightened from the drive down the mountain. He crossed the room and had her in his arms before the first sob broke the silence. "Gypsy?" Bart soothed her as she clung to him, the sobs shaking her slender body.

"You don't understand," she sobbed. "I *have* to do these things. They're my *responsibility*. I have to."

Andrea took a couple of deep breaths, trying to calm herself. It was going to kill her, this warring of her own emotions. She didn't know how to make time for him, to give him what he needed and still meet all the obligations she had. She understood that he had made a choice and it was all right. There was only him. His family didn't need him as hers needed her.

"I'm not angry because you have things you have to do, Gypsy."

Bart wanted to shake her, to make her see that what bothered him wasn't that she had to work. He wanted to tell her again that her family was using her, making her responsible for things she shouldn't have to worry about. He wanted to point out that being a family meant sharing the worry and the good times.

"Then why?"

He also knew now wasn't the time and his words wouldn't penetrate. For whatever reason, Andrea insisted on seeing his denials as statements of not wanting commitment. He would have to try to show her, teach her by deeds, not words.

"Because you were shutting me out. You didn't want to ask for my help again."

"I understand you aren't at a point where you want to deal with all of this, Mr. Collins."

"Why don't you let me decide what I want to deal with and what I don't? I'm perfectly capable of saying no."

"You said you wanted time to watch sunsets and have picnics in warm meadows. I don't have much time now. And I won't until May."

She didn't understand that taking care of her family as she did went past the point of duty. They felt they had the arbitrary right to demand her presence and help. They left her no room of her own. It was no wonder she saw marriage as nothing but work.

"Maybe, if you let me help, you would have more time, Gypsy, for yourself and for us."

She wanted and needed him in her life. She couldn't let go, not easily, not again. "I'll have more time after the wedding." She looked up at him, her eyes bright with still unshed tears. "In fact, I should be free all day tomorrow. There shouldn't be one thing I have to do."

"And I plan to take advantage of it," Bart promised.

# Ten

____

I don't understand you, Bart Collins. I really don't."

Bart smiled across the car. "I know that, Gypsy."

"I thought you were upset because I'm busy all the time, but the first thing you do is accept an invitation to dinner at my mother's house."

Bart pulled over to the curb, put the car into Park and turned to face one very upset witch. Yesterday had not been the time to confront her with the issues that stood between them. She had still had the last-minute details of her sister's wedding to contend with. But today was as good a time as any to start telling her what he saw and what he wanted.

"What did you think I meant, when I told you it was serious, when I followed you clear across the country?"

Andrea shrugged. "I don't know."

"Then I'll explain it. I knew before you left that you were important to me. After you left, I found I didn't have a life. It was empty and incomplete without you." He covered her mouth gently with his hand, as she opened it to protest. "And it wasn't just the sex, though I've never experienced anything before like I do when I make love to you." Slowly he lowered his hand, then gave in to temptation and began to take the pins out of her hair. "It was everything about you, your smile, your independence, even your hesitation to consider marriage."

"You don't believe in commitments and promises," she reminded him quickly.

"I didn't then. You have to understand, Gypsy, I had just spent six years handling almost nothing but divorce cases. All I saw was the pain and anger of broken promises. It colors your thinking after a while. You begin to believe that there is no such thing as love, only acrimony, once the sex wears thin."

She didn't have to believe anything. Just because Bart found it simple to change his beliefs it didn't mean she would. "So, nothing has changed in the world. The divorce rate is still high, people still fight over the car and the dog."

"No, the world hasn't changed," Bart agreed, running his fingers through her hair. "But I have. I went home at Christmas and saw my parents, still happy after forty years of marriage. I saw my sister and her husband, very much in love after six years. I listened to Bill Andrews, who still loves a wife who has been dead for ten years.

"I realized that it wasn't the commitment or promise that I feared, but the pain that comes later. I also realized there is always pain with loving." She had left because there was no commitment between them, and it had hurt. It would hurt again, if he couldn't make her understand. "Life isn't perfect. Relationships aren't perfect. But they are worth working for, worth having. And that's why I followed you, the reason I'm here. To try to work at this relationship we have, the promise we made to each other."

"First, we didn't make any promises," Andrea said. "Second, you may have changed your mind about these things. I haven't. I still don't want the responsibility of marriage."

"Gypsy, every time you are in my arms it's a promise. A promise of our future, of what we can have together." He took her hands into his, aware of the tension she was feeling. "However, before we can achieve that promise, I have to understand why you feel as you do about responsibility. That's why I accepted your mother's invitation today."

"They are my family. I love them. That's why I feel about them as I do."

Bart released her hands and turned back to the steering wheel. "No. It's more than that, sweetheart. You seem to think you have to take care of them. Amanda's wedding is a perfect example. If you'd wanted to help, you would have given her money toward her wedding. Instead you let her use you by paying for the entire affair, and your mother used you by making you feel you had to handle all those details, while she was enjoying the events. For reasons I don't understand, your family seems to think it is your job to support and provide for their needs. They are all grown, Andrea. They can provide for themselves."

"Maybe your family is rich and can afford things easily," Andrea snapped. "Mine isn't. We've had to work for everything we have. Our house, college, the wedding. We've worked for it by sticking together and helping each other."

"No, Gypsy. *You*'ve worked for it and *they*'ve benefited. Who paid *your* way through college? Who helped *you* get your business started? Who would *you* ask for the money for a wedding?"

"I'm the oldest, Bart. I'm the one who could work first, who could help. I'm happy when I can make things easier for them."

"No. They've made you feel responsible and I plan to find out why."

"Why?"

"Because once I understand that part of you, I'll know how to make this relationship work. And it will work, Gypsy," he promised.

Andrea was aware of the warmth of his hand holding hers, even as she sat against the door on her side of the car. She wanted to deny the truth of his words, but today she couldn't. She was too upset about his decision that they would have a relationship. He hadn't used the word "marriage," but everything he had mentioned had certainly sounded as though he was thinking of the long term and forever after.

She didn't want promises from him. She didn't want marriage. He might think it wasn't a responsibility, but it was. Good heavens! There was cooking and cleaning and laundry and bills, and dozens of little, subtle things you never thought of, but which always got in the way. And then there would be children, and the responsibilities would triple. Not only child care but sports, music, school. It was an endless treadmill. She had enough now. She didn't want all that.

Andrea had calmed down by the time Bart turned into her mother's driveway. It had taken her a few minutes, but rational thinking had put things back into perspective. First, dinner with her mother would not show him some mysterious reason for her being "taken advantage of." She wasn't. He would simply see a family that helped each other.

Second, he had said he was serious. "Serious" could mean many things. It didn't necessarily mean marriage, even if he had talked about his parents and his sister. He hadn't gotten serious enough to mention a job, where they would live, or children.

And last, he had no idea what dinner with her mother would be like. An inquisition could sometimes be easier.

Bart knew he had upset Andrea, both with his declaration that he intended to make their relationship work, as well as by his evaluation of her family. He hadn't wanted to upset her, but if she wanted to spend her time in the kitchen, that was fine. It left her mother available for questions.

"Andrea doesn't look like you or either of your other children," Bart said, studying the family pictures that filled one shelf of a bookcase.

"Andrea's like her father."

Bart replaced Andrea's picture. Tina hadn't said, "She looks like her father," rather, "She *is* like." Andrea had never mentioned her father. "Is Mr. MacLarson dead?" There were no pictures of him in the room.

"I have no idea," Tina said. "Nor do I care."

"You're divorced?"

"No."

"Dad left when I was thirteen," Andrea said from the doorway. "The last we heard, he was in Australia. He was going to try sheep farming."

Bart turned toward her, aware of the wistful tone. She still missed her father. "When did you see him last?"

"The day before he left."

Bart crossed the room, taking her into his arms. Seventeen years since she had seen her father. Thirteen was a fragile age to lose a parent.

"Don't feel sorry for Andrea," Tina snapped. "She's much better off without him around."

She had leaned against him until her mother made her announcement, then she straightened, stepping back. "The biscuits are ready and everything is on the table. Why don't we eat now?"

She didn't want him opening these issues, Bart realized. Which meant these were probably the issues he needed to probe. "I feel regret for any person who loses a parent, whatever the cause. Every parent has something to offer a child."

Andrea sighed and tuned out her mother's strident denial that Mac had had any saving graces at all. She had heard her mother's opinion so often, she could recite it by heart. Her father had been irresponsible and unreliable. He had been a dreamer. He had expected life handed to him on a silver platter.

She had good memories of her father, too, things her mother would never mention. "You always forget the good side, Mom." She didn't want Bart Collins thinking Mac had been a lazy bum. He'd just been different. "Dad always had time to read to us at night. He took us on walks and played with us. He made us laugh and sing. He loved all of us very much."

"He taught you silly dreams. He taught you to see the world through his blinders." Tina's voice was hard and cold. "And after he left, Susie took over. Encouraging you in those ridiculous schemes, when you needed to be working."

"What ridiculous schemes?" Bart asked, all too aware of the pain on Andrea's face.

"She wanted to be an anthropologist or an archaeologist," Tina said. "And when I finally talked her out of it, told her how ridiculous it was, Susie tried to undo it all by leaving her that shack and stating she had to stay there a month. Andrea has enough of her father in her that I'm surprised she came back at all."

Bart understood too much. Andrea had become her mother's scapegoat because of her resemblance to her father. She had been castigated by her mother and made to play out the role of penitent, since Mac wasn't around to do it. And Andrea at the vulnerable age of thirteen had believed her parent. To avoid losing the one person she had left, she had cooperated until now she believed it.

"What would have been wrong with her staying in New Mexico?" Bart asked. "She's single. She had no dependents. If that's what she wants, I don't see where it's anyone's business but hers." And mine, he added to himself.

Tina stared at him as if he had spoken in Martian. "Andrea has responsibilities, Bart. She has a business to run, and her family is here. She can't just drop everything and go, as evidently you can."

Andrea excused herself, though neither of them seemed to notice that she left the table. They were locked in verbal combat, each busy trying to prove the other wrong. Sighing, she slipped out the back door and stood on the steps.

Next month it would be spring. The grass would start to turn green, flowers would begin to bloom, and the world would grow warm. She smiled. She hadn't been cold since Mr. Collins had shown up at her office last week. The cold that had bothered her all winter had been an emotional chill, not the weather.

Turning to go back in, she heard the harsh sound of her mother's voice. Bart wasn't going to change Tina's mind, nor was he going to learn any truth that would change her own life. And her mother wasn't going to influence Mr. Collins in any way.

Couldn't they see they were both right? She was as free as Bart said. If she decided to go, she could go. She didn't need anyone's permission. And her mother was right. She did have a family here who needed her. She also had a business that she had worked hard to build, and it wasn't something she would walk away from.

One might think she would have had enough common sense not to fall in love with a man who was tilting at windmills. Why couldn't she be more like Amanda and fall in love with a man with a stable, established career?

Why had she fallen in love at all? She had enough now. She didn't need the added hassles—like today. Bart Collins could have dinner with her mother whenever he liked. She wanted a day to relax after all the work of the wedding. The next two months would be nonstop work. She needed her day off.

Bart watched Andrea through the dining-room window as Tina continued talking. Andrea had inherited at least one trait from her mother—blind stubbornness.

"Mrs. MacLarson, you keep telling me Andrea is irresponsible and flighty. When I look at her, I see a hard-working businesswoman with a successful career. I see a woman who constantly puts other people ahead of herself."

"You see those things because I've pushed," Tina said. "And she's had Julie's stabilizing influence as a business partner. Do you know that not only did she spend a month in New Mexico, she refuses to sell that shack?"

"A wise investment choice," Bart stated.

"I doubt that seriously." Bart saw the calculating gleam in the woman's eyes. "She's keeping it for sentimental reasons. Because it was Susie's."

"This may sound mean, but I'm glad David was working this afternoon," Andrea said as Julie stopped to look at some place mats. "I needed something mindless like this."

"I thought you would be with Bart, or I would have called," Julie said.

"I was." She would rather have been, if she was honest with herself. "I left him and Mom debating the issues of responsibility."

Julie reached for Andrea's hand, giving it a quick squeeze. "He asked about your father."

"Yeah," Andrea admitted with a sigh. "And then Mom brought Susie into it. I don't think either one of them noticed when I left. I just walked out the back door."

Julie nodded her understanding and tossed the place mats back. "Come on. Time for some tea and girl talk." She laughed knowingly. "Though if I know Bart at all, he'll be sitting on your doorstep or mine."

"No. He'll be using all his courtroom tricks to persuade Mom."

As they were heading out of the store, Julie stopped to admire a lacy gown. "This would look lovely on you."

Andrea stroked the creamy lace and satin. "It wouldn't stay on long enough to make it worth the money."

"Definitely time for some girl talk," Julie stated, taking the gown from the rack and heading for the cashier. "My treat."

"I knew you'd go into matchmaking overdrive," Andrea protested.

"Someone has to, Andrea, or your mother will have you married to some dull, boring workaholic like your sister just married."

Two hours later Andrea was curled on Julie's sofa, munching a chocolate chip cookie that Julie said David had made.

"Bart cooks, too. I wonder if he bakes cookies?"

"Good. We'll let the men take care of us, especially during April."

"That doesn't bother you?"

"No. Why should it?"

Andrea shrugged. "I can take care of myself."

"So can I," Julie said. "So when David does it, it's because I'm being pampered and loved. It's wonderful. Your problem is that you aren't used to being pampered. If Bart wants to do it, let him."

"But, Julie, I don't know what he wants. I don't even know why he's here."

"I want you, Gypsy. And I'm here because this is where you are."

Andrea turned at the sound of Bart's deep voice. He was standing in the doorway with David, his eyes brooding, almost angry. She bit her lower lip, knowing she shouldn't have walked out.

"I found this guy skulking around our front," David said. "He swore he was looking for my wife's house, so I brought him in." He crossed the room to Julie and kissed her soundly. "Why is another man looking for you, my dear?"

Julie laughed at the teasing. "Because I'm beautiful and sexy, but I feel sure this man was hoping to find Andrea. I always make it clear to my admirers that I'm a married woman now."

"You better," David warned. Smiling, he turned to Bart. "Why don't you stay for dinner?"

Bart knew he needed all the support he could get. Gypsy needed to see that he fitted into her world in every way. "We'd love to. Thank you."

"Great," David said. "Come on in and sit down, Bart. What can I get you to drink? Come on, Julie, let's see what we can throw together for a meal."

Andrea watched Julie and David leave the room arm in arm. She was aware that Bart had not taken his eyes off her.

"You walked out," he said.

"I—" She wasn't going to apologize. She hadn't wanted to go. "I've heard it all before." She glanced at his rumpled hair and loosened tie. "You survived the inquisition."

"Of course."

Andrea realized she was the odd man out as the evening progressed. Bart fitted in as if he were the old friend, not her.

But no matter what Andrea thought, she wasn't ready to lose Bart. She readily agreed to returning to his hotel for the night.

"This isn't very practical," Andrea said several hours later. She hung her dress in the closet and set the overnight case on the dresser.

"Gypsy, I wouldn't fit in your bed."

Andrea grinned, imagining his length wedged into her standard-size bed. But staying in a hotel wasn't reasonable, either.

"I could get a king-size bed. The bedroom would be cramped, but it would fit."

Bart dropped the shoe he had just removed and stared across the room. She was making space for him in her life. It had been an offer to share her home. His heart swelled with joy as he crossed the room and took her slender form into his arms.

"Are you suggesting I live with you, Miss MacLarson?"

"I guess I am," she admitted. "Will you?"

"Starting tomorrow." Gently he brushed her hair back. "And I thought I would have to force my attentions on you," he teased.

"You are quite forceful enough, Mr. Collins."

"I can be gentle, too," he whispered against her mouth.

Andrea let his gentle lovemaking take her soaring to ecstasy, only to float back to earth in his embrace. She still wasn't sure she wanted marriage and a family, but she did want Bart Collins in her life. For as long as he wanted to be there.


Bart fitted into her life easily. He made it fuller, richer and more rewarding. It was still hectic, but there was more time for herself and for them.

As the work load at the office increased, he was there more and more. He ran errands, picked up lunch, made copies, anything to ease the hectic pace for her and Julie. Sometimes she teased him about putting him onto the payroll. He always laughed, but refused.

He taught her how to be pampered and cared for. He would fix a hot bath and rub her shoulders after a long day. When she thought she was too tired to eat he always found something to tempt her. He made her relax and get away for a few hours each week; a movie, a ride in the country or simply a long walk through the park.

As she learned to take, she also learned to give from the heart. She would fix him a meat and potatoes meal he loved or a special dessert. She learned to make time, sometimes dragging him off at lunch, often just to take him home and spend those precious moments in his arms.

There were disagreements, usually about her family. And Andrea couldn't help but worry about his jobless state, even though he contributed his share and more of their expenses. It wasn't perfect, but she was content with the way it was.

Bart was amazed at the changes in Andrea. As the weeks passed she opened up, becoming more loving and giving than she had been. She learned how to let him take care of her and even learned to ask him when she needed help. The sexy witch he had known in New Mexico blossomed. He never tired of her, always ready, always needing her again.

Bart knew he was in love. Andrea was the woman he wanted to spend the rest of his life with, the woman he wanted to mother his children and grow old beside.

There was only one major problem. Her family.

"Gypsy, we're going to be late."

"I'm almost ready." Andrea brushed mascara onto her lashes, grabbing her earrings and purse at the same time. "Ready, I think." She twirled once for Bart's inspection, aware of his impatience.

"I imagine they require shoes."

Andrea dashed to the closet and found one high-heeled black shoe. The other took a minute longer to locate. It was under the bed. "Now I'm ready."

She almost had to run to keep up with Bart as he strode toward the door. She knew he was angry. She was running late, because her mother had had a flat tire and called her. Amanda was having a dinner party, and Rory was out of town. Bart had asked her not to go, but she couldn't leave her mother stranded at the mall. She had called the auto club and gone to wait with her mother. Just as Bart opened the door, the phone began to ring again.

"Don't answer it, Andrea. Get in the car."

"But it might be important."

"Like another flat tire." He took her arm. "We're already late. We either go now or we don't go at all."

"You could have gone with me and changed the tire. Then it wouldn't have taken so long." The phone shrilled yet again.

Bart tugged her through the doorway. "Your mother could have called the auto club all by herself. She didn't need you to hold her hand."

Andrea jerked her arm free. "That's not fair, Bart. Mom wasn't raised to have all the responsibility. She gets upset and doesn't think."

"So she raised you to handle everything. Always responsible. Always reliable."

"You didn't have someone walk out on you and leave you with three children to feed and care for."

"Your mother has had seventeen years to learn. She's had seventeen years to get over it and go on with her life. Instead, she spent all those years making you mother and father to the point you can't even go out without a guilty conscience."

"Maybe it's you who has the guilty conscience. Maybe you feel guilty because you wouldn't help."

Bart pulled the door shut on the still ringing phone. "Do you realize how many times we're late, or how often our supper gets cold, while you take care of your family?"

"Are you jealous of the time I spend with my family?" Andrea demanded.

"Jealous? No, Andrea. I'm sick of it. I'm sick of the way you're being used. And I'm sick of having our plans interrupted. I'm tired of your lectures on responsibility, when all that's happening is your family being inconsiderate." Bart looked at his watch and swore softly. "Go answer the damned phone. The evening is ruined, anyhow."

Andrea watched Bart stride toward the bedroom before reaching for the phone, which was still ringing.

"Amanda? What's wrong? Why are you crying?"

Bart heard the words with a sense of inevitability. Andrea would never have a life of her own or be willing to take the next step, unless she learned to say no. And she would never say no unless she could see the difference between doing her duty and being used.

Pulling the tickets from his pocket, he threw them onto the dresser. The ballet was to have been a surprise. He should have known that he wouldn't get her out of Columbus in time to get to Atlanta.

Andrea replaced the receiver and walked slowly down the hall toward the bedroom. She stopped in the doorway. Bart sat on the end of the bed, head down, looking almost dejected.

"I'm sorry."

"What was Amanda's problem?"

"Her dinner was a disaster. They ended up having to go out, and Dudley was angry."

Bart glanced up at her. "And I bet she wants you to teach her how to cook." The startled look on her face told him he had hit the mark. "And you said yes, of course."

"It won't take that much time," Andrea said. "Just a few evenings."

Bart shook his head and stood. "It's always something, isn't it. Flat tires. Burned dinners. A screwed-up checkbook. And only you can fix it."

"Bart, they're—"

"Your family. I know. Don't you find it strange that other families manage? Don't you find it odd that Julie doesn't go through this? Or me?"

"My family's closer than most."

"Your family is more dependent than any I've ever seen in my life."

Andrea watched, her hands turning icy with dread, as Bart pulled his suitcase from the closet and began putting clothes into it.

"Bart?" She didn't want him to go. She didn't want to lose him. "Mr. Collins, please don't go." If it came to making a choice, she would try. "I'll tell Amanda no tomorrow."

Bart paused and turned to her. "No, Gypsy. I don't want to come between you and your family. You were honest about one thing. You don't have time for more."

Andrea reached out. "I'll make time. I'll—"

"No. You have to learn without me. They use you, Andrea, and you let them. When you're ready to stand up for yourself, I'll be back."

"Where will you be?"

"I don't know," Bart said, snapping the case shut. "Watching a sunset somewhere, I imagine."

Andrea didn't know it was possible to hurt as much as she did and still keep living. When she tried to talk to Julie, she got no support at all. Julie sided with Bart completely. Andrea felt that no one in the world understood.

She functioned on automatic for the next several days, going through the routines by rote. Only at night did she give in to the pain. The king-size bed felt as wide as a continent and as empty as a desert. She tried to convince herself he had gone because he didn't want responsibility, but it didn't stop the tears or ease the pain in her heart.

Julie might not have been sympathetic to her point of view, but she was understanding about how she was feeling. Several times she and David insisted Andrea come over for the evening, practically dragging her out of the office.

But even there her mother found her, and as usual, her mother needed something. Andrea honestly didn't think she could handle it. And when she overheard David say he was surprised Bart had lasted as long as he had with her family, Andrea was forced to step back and take a new look at herself and her relationships.

When Amanda appeared on her doorstep later in the week, she knew she couldn't do as she had promised. "Oh, Amanda, I'm sorry. I forgot you were coming. Can we do this another night?"

"Dudley has invited another couple over tomorrow night. I've got to fix something decent this time."

"Let Dudley fix it," Andrea snapped.

"What's the matter with you?" Amanda asked as she hung her coat.

Andrea burst into tears. "Mr. Collins left."

"Oh. Well, you knew he would. He didn't have a job or anything."

"Since when is a man's job the only basis for a relationship?" Andrea snapped, surprising even herself with her vehemence.

Amanda turned and looked at her. "You have not fallen in love with *him*, have you?"

"Yes, I have," Andrea admitted. "Very much so."

"Well, I'm sorry," Amanda said. "I really am. But you should have known it wouldn't work. I mean he wasn't stable and responsible and reliable. He was bound to leave."

Andrea stared at her sister as she sat down and pulled out a cookbook. It wasn't that Amanda's tone had been recriminating or cold. It was the words she had used, almost identical to those she herself had used when talking to Julie. Amanda was simply saying what had been drilled into their heads since they were children. Responsibility and duty before all else. Andrea helped Amanda with the recipe, her mind on a dozen other thoughts.

As she crawled into the empty bed that night, she admitted Mr. Collins had been right. She did let herself be used by her family, all of them, from her mother to Amanda.

The work pace doubled as they neared the April tax deadline. Andrea began to find her family's demands insufferable. They all knew how upset and how busy she was, yet they didn't hesitate to call for something. She also learned that it wasn't easy to say no. Sometimes she didn't know if she was shedding tears over her broken heart, or because she was upsetting her family with her new limits.

April 15 came and went. The worst was over. Not only would the work load start to decrease to a manageable level, she was also starting to feel comfortable saying no. She was finally beginning to understand what Mr. Collins had meant about taking responsibility too far.

And with that came a deeper understanding of her mother and father. She had done exactly as her mother had, trying to turn Bart Collins into what she thought he should be, rather than accepting him for the man he was, loving, kind, caring, warm—wonderful.

She was learning to say no and had begun to understand many things, but she had no idea where Bart Collins had gone or which sunset he might be watching.

She could only pray he'd keep his promise to return. Until then, she'd have no way of telling him what she'd come to learn.

# Eleven

———

Andrea was sitting at her desk, paying more attention to the swaying leaves on the tree than the data computer terminal, when Sue announced her two o'clock appointment. Andrea turned back to her desk and straightened a file before pulling a fresh legal pad into place and laying a pencil on top of it. The door opened and she looked up.

For a long moment she sat stunned as her eyes drank in the figure filling her doorway. His height, the breadth of his shoulders, the beautiful, dark brown eyes. Her trance lasted only long enough to confirm it was him, before she ran around the desk and threw herself into his arms.

"Oh, Mr. Collins, you came back. You really came back. I've missed you so much." She inhaled the clean, masculine scent as her muscles absorbed the heat of his body.

"Do you greet all your clients this way, Miss Mac-Larson?"

"Client?" Only then did she realize he was dressed in a business suit and carrying a briefcase. "You're only here as a client?'' She fought against the tears and tried to pull herself together as he closed the door.

"Gypsy."

She was pulled into his arms and kissed thoroughly. She couldn't have said who was clinging to whom the harder.

"I missed you, Gypsy. God, yes, I've missed you." He kissed her again, holding her in an almost crushing embrace. "But right now I am here as a potential client."

Very gently he set her down. Confused, Andrea allowed him to lead her back to her desk. Once she was seated, he sat down opposite her.

"I'm opening an office in town," he said. "Erikson's firm has recommended you highly. Basically it would be to handle payroll and taxes for me."

Andrea couldn't seem to grasp what he was saying. One minute she was in his arms, and the next he was telling her he was opening an office and wanted to hire her firm. Why was he doing this? Why was he going to start working now?

"Why are you opening an office?"

"I know a woman who is very special to me. She feels it important that her man be employed."

Her love grew even more than before. He was doing it because of her. But Andrea had learned that it was wrong to change another person. She loved Bart Collins for who he was, not what he was. She also knew he would never be happy unless it was something he truly wanted.

"Bart, we need to talk."

"We will. Later. I'd like to get this business out of the way first. Can your firm handle another account?"

"Yes, but—"

"Good," he interrupted. Before she realized what he was going to do, he reached across her desk and pressed the intercom. "Sue, Andrea will be out the remainder of the day." He released the button and looked at her. "Get your purse and let's go."

"Bart, I can't just walk out."

"Sure you can." Ignoring her protests, he ushered her out of the office to his car. "You said we needed to talk, and now is the perfect time."

At least he hadn't totally changed, Andrea thought as she followed him out of the office. She paused beside his car.

"Bart, I have learned how to say no."

"I know you have. Are you going to tell me no?"

Andrea shook her head and slipped inside the car. She wanted to see him too much to tell him no.

"How did you know I had learned?" she asked as he slid behind the wheel.

"I had my sources."

"Remind me to send Julie some flowers."

Bart chuckled, his eyes filled with laughter.

Andrea watched with a mixture of curiosity and trepidation as Bart drove into a newer subdivision and pulled into the driveway of a modern house. Bart urged her from the car and inside, only saying that he wanted her to see it. The downstairs had a formal living room and dining room, as well as a great room with knotty pine paneling and a huge, fieldstone fireplace.

"It reminds me of my house in New Mexico," Andrea said, falling in love with the room and the open kitchen beyond. Large windows filled the area with light and overlooked a spacious yard.

"I thought it would. I'm thinking about buying it."

Andrea turned and stared at him. "Mr. Collins, you can't do that."

"Why not? I like the house. You haven't seen the bedrooms yet, but there are four. The master bedroom has a fireplace, too."

Andrea looked around the spacious great room and then back to the man she loved. "Earlier you said you were opening an office because of me." He nodded. "That's wrong. You won't be happy, if that's why you're doing it. It's not important to me if you have a job."

"It's not?"

Andrea looked at the floor for a moment. She had changed, and it wasn't going to be easy to convince him. "No, it's not, not anymore. Being with you is the most important thing."

"Being with you is important to me too, Gypsy. That's why I want this house."

Andrea wasn't sure she was ready to deal with the implications of that statement. "Tell me about your new practice."

Bart smiled, leading her to the hearth and sitting down. "I needed the time off to think and put my life in perspective. Now I'm ready to do what I want." Bart gently pulled her down beside him and held her in his arms. "Bill Andrews once told me there were a lot of people who needed a lawyer but couldn't afford one. Half of my practice will be devoted to assisting those people. I'll be working through the public defender's office, as well as accepting clients who need help, but can't afford the fees from other firms."

Andrea glanced around the room. "You won't make a lot of money doing that." The house wasn't a mansion, but it wasn't inexpensive, either.

"Is the money that important to you, Gypsy?"

Andrea turned in his arms so that she could see his face. "No. The money isn't important. You are." She reached up to stroke his beard. "Mr. Collins, are you sure this is what you want? Will the new job and this house make you happy?"

"Everyone needs a job that is satisfying. And everyone needs a place to call home. Hotels aren't very practical."

Andrea stood and paced across the empty room before coming back to Bart. "In New Mexico you kept telling me Susie wanted me to learn something. I didn't learn then. I learned it later, from you."

"What did you learn, sweetheart?"

"That it's okay to be yourself. It's not wrong to dream or try new things. That it's all right to say no." She half smiled. "I'm still working on that one. But most importantly, it's wrong to try to change people. I think that's what my mother did. Rather than loving my father for the man he was, she kept trying to make him into the man she thought he should be." Andrea reached up and stroked his beard. "I love you just as you are, Mr. Collins. I don't want to change you."

"Would you say that last part again, Gypsy?"

"I don't want to change you."

"No, the other."

Andrea looked into his brown eyes, her heart beating so hard that she could barely speak. "I love you."

"Oh, Gypsy, I love you." Bart swung her into his arms, his mouth claiming hers. "I love you," he murmured as he dropped kisses over her face.

"You don't have to do any of this, Mr. Collins."

Bart looked down, noting the golden flecks in her eyes. He loved the way her eyes changed into warm heat with his touch.

"I want the law practice." He framed her face in his hands. "I want the house for us. But most of all I want you. I want to share the rest of my life with you."

Andrea opened her mouth to speak and stopped. She glanced around the room and then back to Bart Collins. "Was that a marriage proposal?"

"Yes."

"Oh."

"For a shared life, Gypsy. I want to *share* my life with you. Will you?"

She knew he meant those words. It would be shared. Not only the good, but the bad and the everyday things.

"Yes, I will, if you promise to yell at me when I start trying to do it all."

Bart chuckled, lifting her into his arms. "I think I have a much better way to stop you," he promised, starting up the stairs. "One I plan to put into practice right now."

"Where are we going?"

"To the bedroom," Bart said.

"Is this the way you plan to keep me in line?" she asked as she fumbled with his tie.

"Yes," Bart promised, his voice rough with passion.

Her dress slipped from her shoulders to fall in a puddle at her feet.

"Woman, you wear too many clothes."

"Just something else I need to learn," she agreed as she lost herself in the magic of his embrace.

"We'll learn together from now on," Bart promised as he eased her down.

\*     \*     \*     \*     \*

# Diamond Jubilee Collection

## It's our 10th Anniversary... and *you* get a present!

This collection of early Silhouette Romances features novels written by three of your favorite authors:

**ANN MAJOR**—*Wild Lady*
**ANNETTE BROADRICK**—*Circumstantial Evidence*
**DIXIE BROWNING**—*Island on the Hill*

* These Silhouette Romance titles were first published in the early 1980s and have not been available since!

* Beautiful Collector's Edition bound in antique green simulated leather to last a lifetime!

* Embossed in gold on the cover and spine!

This special collection will not be sold in retail stores and is only available through this exclusive offer.
Look for details in all Silhouette series published in June, July and August.

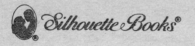

**Silhouette Special Edition®**

Appearing in October
for a return engagement, Nora Roberts's
bestselling 1988 miniseries featuring

# THE O'HURLEYS!
## Nora Roberts

**Book 1** **THE LAST HONEST WOMAN** *Abby's Story*
**Book 2** **DANCE TO THE PIPER** *Maddy's Story*
**Book 3** **SKIN DEEP** *Chantel's Story*

And making his debut in a brand-new title, a very special leading man... Trace O'Hurley!

**Book 4** **WITHOUT A TRACE** *Trace's Tale*

In 1988, Nora Roberts introduced THE O'HURLEYS!—a close-knit family of entertainers whose early travels spanned the country. The beautiful triplet sisters and their mysterious brother each experience the triumphant joy and passion only true love can bring, in four books you will remember long after the last pages are turned.

Don't miss this captivating miniseries in October—a special collector's edition available wherever paperbacks are sold.

**Double your reading pleasure this fall with two Award of Excellence titles written by two of your favorite authors.**

*Available in September*

**DUNCAN'S BRIDE**
by Linda Howard
Silhouette Intimate Moments #349

Mail-order bride Madelyn Patterson was nothing like what Reese Duncan expected—and everything he needed.

*Available in October*

**THE COWBOY'S LADY**
by Debbie Macomber
Silhouette Special Edition #626

The Montana cowboy wanted a little lady at his beck and call—the ''lady'' in question saw things differently....

These titles have been selected to receive a special laurel—the Award of Excellence. Look for the distinctive emblem on the cover. It lets you know there's something truly wonderful inside! DUN-1

# COMING SOON...

For years Harlequin and Silhouette novels have been taking readers places—but only in their imaginations.

This fall look for PASSPORT TO ROMANCE, a promotion that could take you around the corner or around the world!

**Watch for it in September!**

★